CROSSING THE CITY

Also by Michel Tremblay

Desrosiers Diaspora

Crossing the Continent

Chronicles of the Plateau Mont-Royal

The Fat Woman Next Door Is Pregnant
Thérèse and Pierrette and the Little Hanging Angel
The Duchess and the Commoner
News from Édouard
The First Quarter of the Moon
A Thing of Beauty

All available from Talonbooks

The Desrosiers Diaspora

CROSSING THE CITY

A Novel

MICHEL TREMBLAY
Translated by Sheila Fischman

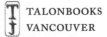

TALONBOOKS
VANCOUVER

Talonbooks
278 East First Avenue, Vancouver, British Columbia, Canada v5T 1A6

www.talonbooks.com

First printing: 2014

Typeset in Adobe Caslon
Printed and bound in Canada on 100% post-consumer recycled paper
Interior and cover design by Typesmith

Cover painting by Adrien Hébert, *Sainte-Catherine St. Montreal* (detail), 1926
The McCuaig Collection
Laurentian University Museum and Art Centre
The Art Gallery of Sudbury

Talonbooks gratefully acknowledges the financial support of the Canada Council for the Arts, the Government of Canada through the Canada Book Fund, and the Province of British Columbia through the British Columbia Arts Council and the Book Publishing Tax Credit.

This work was originally published in French as *La traversée de la ville* by Leméac Éditeur (Montreal, Quebec) and Actes Sud (Paris, France) in 2008. We acknowledge the financial support of the Government of Canada, through the National Translation Program, for our translation activities.

LIBRARY AND ARCHIVES CANADA CATALOGUING IN PUBLICATION

Tremblay, Michel, 1942–
[Traversée de la ville. English]

Crossing the city / Michel Tremblay ; translated by Sheila Fischman.

(The Desrosiers diaspora)
Translation of: La traversée de la ville.
Issued in print and electronic formats.
ISBN 978-0-88922-893-1 (pbk.).—ISBN 978-0-88922-894-8 (epub)

I. Fischman, Sheila, translator II. Title. III. Title: Traversée de la ville. English

PS8539.R47T67713 2014   C843'.54   C2014-903253-6
                                                  C2014-903254-4

Once again, the names are true but everything around them is sheer invention.

— M. T.

Give me back what is mine,
Gods of Tartary!

— ALESSANDRO STRIGGIO
Orpheus by Claudio Monteverdi

For Lily, Kim, and Théo,
in the hope that someday
they will read this book

PRELUDE

PROVIDENCE, RHODE ISLAND

On the morning when she realized she was very likely pregnant for the fourth time, Maria Rathier did not go to work at the Nicholson File cotton mill where she'd been earning her living – barely – for nearly five years. Instead, she left her house, walked all the way across the city, going along Dorrance Street as she did every day but walking right past the red-brick factory shrouded in lint, and took a seat on the bank of the Providence River, on the very bench were Simon had asked her to marry him.

Simon had been reported missing at sea years before. She hoped he was dead because a few things about him weren't quite respectable. Though his relatives, the Rathier clan, French from France and living in Rhode Island since the end of the Civil War, still hoped he'd come back, comical and sly as ever, Maria knew that if he wasn't dead he'd most likely started a new life somewhere farther south, in Virginia say, where he'd admitted to her one day that he had other "relatives," meaning another woman or women. Or a second family. Good for him. And for her. She had loved a man who didn't exist, an individual intent on seducing her, of enclosing her within four walls with her children, while he – master mariner, adventurer, man of the seas, seafarer – sailed in every direction, slapped his thighs when he thought he'd told a good one. And chewed on his meerschaum like an old sea dog, his blue eyes focused on the horizon and his handsome wrinkles creased by the irritating smile of a self-confident man, a swaggering provincial. At the same time, he had needed a nest where he could deposit his eggs and the whole wide world where he could be free. Finally he chose the whole wide world and left – for good.

When she realized he wouldn't be coming back, Maria had felt not happy but relieved in a strange but familiar way, as if the defeatism that seemed natural in her family – the Saskatchewan

5

Desrosiers way out there to the north and west, at the other end of the continent, Crees who were definitely brave but struck with a kind of melancholy – had led them to a fatalism they considered to be both inevitable and invincible. To her great regret, she'd had to send away her three little girls, and now they were with her mother in Saskatchewan, because Maria couldn't meet their needs, and the Rathier family, tight-knit as they appeared to be, refused to help. Which had been proof that there was no hope of Simon's coming home, that all of it – the overly flaunted hope, the diehard optimism – was merely a smokescreen to hide their own relief because, finally, Simon had been no more generous with them than with her and, in the end, they were fed up with him too and his absence weighed less than they claimed. With her children gone, Maria had thought she would die of grief but she'd held on, promising to take them back some day, all four of them happy here in Providence, or back in Canada, but not in Saskatchewan, especially not in the little village in the back of beyond called Maria that had witnessed her birth and inspired her name, but where she'd felt so cramped. She hadn't left on a whim, ranting and raving about the place only to come back twelve years later, head hanging and shoulders hunched. No, to Montreal maybe. Or Quebec City. In any case to a place where they spoke French, even the spoiled variety born of the mix of Old French inherited from the seventeenth-century settlers and the English now omnipresent in North America, that way of talking that had amused her so much in the past when visitors from Quebec with their loud and colourful way of talking came to visit the Desrosiers in Saskatchewan. (Here too, in Providence, French was spoken. But less and less.) Even the Rathiers tried to imitate the New England accent, saying *Baston* instead of *Boston* and *tomahto* instead of *tomāto*. This was the United States and they did their best to live as Americans: Tremblays gradually became Trembles, Dubucs Dubuques, Desrosiers Desrogers. The new generation spoke a broken French and you heard more people speaking English in their homes, though the women had decided when they came there to live that the French language would predominate.) Yes, she was going to take back her daughters, emigrate, resume her family name, Desrosiers, and forget those five years at a mill where the employees were treated like slaves in a hypocritical country that advocated freedom even as it was imposing the opposite on its workers.

But after years of voluntary widowhood and attacks of depression from which she'd had trouble extricating herself, she who used to be so cheerful, so alive, she'd met this Mondirut Rambert, kind, sensitive, mild-mannered, a gentleman older than Maria, who respected and looked after her instead of treating her the way Simon had. She had got back something of an appetite for life, her good humour too, she'd even started to imagine a possible future with him and her three daughters, even though he was nearly old enough to be their grandfather, but now destiny was turning against her once again. Monsieur Rambert – she never used his first name – hadn't talked about having a child with her or about marriage, promising her nothing but protection and affection – how would he take this news? She had put up with the insults of her husband Simon's family who suspected that she wasn't content with a night on the town with Monsieur Rambert, that their relationship was "guilty" as the husband hadn't been declared officially dead, she had blushed as her neighbours looked on when the old gentleman rang the bell at her little apartment on Fountain Street, even hung her head – she who normally was so rebellious – when the neighbourhood women had called her a slut. Would she go so far as to display her pregnant self to all the eyes in the village without going to the altar of the little parish church she didn't attend? And what about him, would he abandon her as soon as she admitted she was expecting his child, like in the cheap novels from France that the women traded with one another on the sly because they were reputed to be scandalous, that they revelled in with guilty pleasure while hiding them from their husbands and children? Would she be shouted down and isolated in a community that itself was already shouted down and isolated? She'd arrived here singing twelve years earlier with hope in her heart, finally free after a childhood fed on ignorance in the depths of a province where mediocrity ruled, and now, after so many attempts to be just a little bit happy, there she was slumped on a park bench, distraught and confused, disarmed in the face of such a flagrant injustice – the unwelcome baby – that was going to change the course of her life.

She cried on her bench, she berated destiny, she walked back and forth along the shore, waving her arms and talking aloud to herself, calling herself every name in the book, cursed the goddamn men who were always guilty of everything bad, all the time; then she collapsed again on the wooden bench, nauseated, with the first symptoms of a migraine boring into her head.

The end of Indian summer. It had been very hot for three days, an autumn cut in two by blasts of wind from the south; New England had exploded in golds, yellows, reds, even the Providence River had seemed less frigid, some mischievous souls had even ventured into the water on the preceding Sunday afternoon, sending out cries of horror while observers looked on, beaming. In a few hours the wind would change, the clouds would sail in from the west, the leaves would begin to fall, pirouetting, a rain of colour. The last week of October, the papers had said, would mark the definitive death of all hope of fine weather and in its place a grey, cold, rainy November. Already, a hint of coolness to come travelled over the skin, and Maria, feeling a shiver in advance, sensed she was liable to come down with a cold or the flu if she stayed there too long.

But go where? There was no question of going to work, and coming home depressed her nearly as much. She did up her jacket, stuffed her hands in her pockets, stretched her legs out on the gravel path that followed the riverbank.

Just opposite, on the other side of the Providence River that cut the city in two, the construction of Brown University was nearly complete, its opening announced for the following year. An enormous building site, noisy hive of road workers, gardeners, painters putting the final touch to the temple of knowledge erected across from the temples of trade: cotton mills, all kinds of machinery, silverware, where every day tens of thousands of badly paid workers sweated like her. Maria watched them work, trying to think of nothing, to keep her mind blank, to use the trick she had named "look elsewhere," which means ignoring everything that's going badly, forgetting pain and sorrow, and that had been useful so often. She quickly realized this time, however, that the trick would simply not work. How could she forget that feeling of terror, the beginning of panic, the reason, above all, for her feeling of helplessness, and the impossible situation in which she found herself all of a sudden and couldn't see how she could get out of.

Unless …

That's what she had wanted to avoid thinking about for a few hours, she knows that, it was spinning in her head, it wanted to rise to the surface of her consciousness, and she did all she could to avoid facing up to it because she didn't want to become a murderess.

Yes, of course, Madame Bergeron could help.

The abortionist, the *angel maker* as they said.

Tons of stories, each more horrible than the others made the rounds of the neighbourhood about Madame Bergeron: there was talk of butchery, of bloody knitting needles, of pale women coming out of her place bent double, shrieking like madwomen and holding their bellies with both hands; there was talk of an ugly, fat, sadistic woman, a criminal maybe, who used her status of *angel maker* to punish in her own way those who had sinned. It was said that she's a descendant of the famous witches of Salem – after all, Salem's not that far away – while others have actually claimed to have seen her walking along Dorrance Street in the middle of the night, a broom trailing behind her. They dared not claim they'd seen her criss-crossing the sky, cawing like a crow, but it was clearly implied, and women who realized they were pregnant and didn't want it thought longer and longer before availing themselves of her services.

Maria places her hand on her stomach and the image that's been slowly killing her for so many years comes back: her three children – Rhéauna, Béa, Alice – waving her a sad goodbye through the lowered window of a train bound for a journey that would take them to the other end of the world, to the village she had left and sworn never to return to and away to which she found herself obliged to send her offspring. Because of poverty. Of fate. Of the goddamn bad luck that seems to follow her whenever she tries to make a life that is bearable if not normal. It's imprinted in her head like an old yellowed photo and her memory of the distraught faces of her daughters tears her heart to pieces.

Look elsewhere yet again? Act as if none of it existed, neither the irrevocable past nor the present with no apparent way out? Throw back her head and laugh? Throw her head back, possibly; but laugh?

A slight shiver.

She straightens up, rubbing her arms. The workers on the other shore have put their shirts back on despite the perspiration drenching them, because they know that the end of Indian summer is hypocritical and it's easy to catch your death. Actually, that might be the solution: to catch her death of cold. A good attack of double pneumonia that would settle everything. She leans against the guardrail that runs along the riverbank, rests her head on the handrail. Nausea keeps her there for a few minutes. Pneumonia, though, would kill two. Right there, right now, at this very moment, she'd have agreed to die, to forget, but the little thing that has just made her bend double beside the river doesn't deserve to be kept from coming to term, from producing its first little cry, from opening its arms to life.

No Madame Bergeron then, no knitting needle, no egg pierced when barely fertilized.

But what? And where?

Maria leaves the riverside then, goes back to the Dorrance Street hill that makes a bend to the left before arriving at her neighbourhood – the poor district – some distance from the wealthier precinct with its store windows full of food and goods that women like her could never afford. As she walks past the Nicholson File cotton mill, she doesn't even turn her head to look. It's over, all that. She has no idea what will become of her but she does know she'll never go back to that infernal machine, to its heat and noise she's put up with for so many years, the huge wood-and-metal structure that flattened bales of cotton, mixed them with all sorts of stinking and dangerous liquids, and left them to dry before beating, stretching, or spinning them in yet another, equally infernal machine.

Fountain Street is deserted. The women, those not working in a factory at any rate, are busy at their housework while their men sweat bricks in unfit and dirty workshops. No red trees or brown ones here, just a beaten-earth street that would soon turn into a muddy river with the first autumn rain, and wooden sidewalks that were very nearly rotten and stank of cat pee and dog shit. The neighbourhood had been promised asphalt for years now, and concrete sidewalks, but so far only electricity and running water had been put in, the roadwork having stopped for no apparent reason – though it was better than nothing but a lot less than what was needed. People kept their houses clean and themselves well-groomed and tidy in vain; they knew they'd get dirty as soon as they were out the door. And would be judged for their muddy boots and soiled hems.

On her way into the apartment, Maria Rathier has the impression that she is entering someone else's space. What surrounds her means nothing to her, suddenly she doesn't recognize her furniture or the way the apartment is arranged or the few ornaments assembled over the years. She has been there for more than twelve years and nothing looks like it is hers. Nothing of her personality or her taste can be seen. Those curtains on the living-room windows, had she really made them from fabric she'd chosen herself? Had she really bought that hideous sagging sofa flanked by two ghastly mismatched armchairs? Stuff – an assortment of meerschaum pipes, a wine-red armchair she'd always hated, a hole in the kitchen wall, the result of a fit of anger and never repaired – reminds her of Simon, his shouts, his unwashed-fisherman smell – but where does she fit in? Had she done her best all the time she'd been here to "look elsewhere" to the point of forgetting to live? Hardly. With her daughters she'd been happy. Nana's seriousness, Béa's laugh, the curious expression of her baby, Alice, whom she hadn't had time to get to know well ...

She makes herself a cup of black tea but it's too strong and she has to throw it in the sink because it makes her nausea even worse. She has the vague impression that she is sitting beside herself and no longer knows that person who nonetheless was her. Maria sees herself in profile, so thin, holding a cup of tea, a woman disconcerted and lost, who no longer knows if she should struggle or give up and stay, prostrate forever.

She runs herself a bath. The second one that day. Her tub is old, dented, a big thing that used to be enamelled, now with a rusty plug and dripping taps – the landlord had claimed he couldn't install a new bathroom and he'd bought up rich people's scrap – but it is the only place where for some time she's been able to find a certain peace. She takes the big bar of lime-blossom soap from the medicine chest where she keeps it for important occasions – when Monsieur Rambert is coming or when she is planning an evening out downtown – and lets herself soak for a good half-hour in cold water warmed with a few kettles of hot water she's boiled on the coal stove.

Then she thinks about her two sisters living in Montreal: Teena, the happiest of the Desrosiers girls, selling shoes in a big store on Mont-Royal Avenue, and Tititte, the eldest, who had followed her husband to London, over there on the other side of the Atlantic, and then come back a few months later because she was homesick. Without her husband. But not divorced either because the Catholic church didn't permit it any more in England than in Canada. Protestants, the vast majority in England, had the right to divorce, as in Canada – but not Catholics. And Ernest, the eldest, the only male in the family, attached to the Montreal branch of the Mounted Police – the first part-Indian in the country's history to be accepted in the elite police force and who is so proud of it, even though they never sent him out on the beat and his work consisted of juggling paperwork – he might be able to help her. Her family, her brother and sisters anyway, had all gone to Montreal; she alone stayed behind, out of pride or stubbornness. She had left their village, yelling that she hated them, never wanted to see them again; she'd never gotten in touch with them and they were the ones, each in turn, who had tracked her down to Providence and got back in touch with her. Letters had come to her, tinged with surprising tenderness. There was no reference to forgiving or forgetting, only to how they missed her, to how indestructible were their family ties, to the possibility of a reunion. Ernest had even left a phone number. He had a telephone! He must be making money hand over fist with the Mounties! Finally, after weeks of hesitation, she placed the call. He'd been pleasant, even affectionate; he had told her that he knew through their parents, who looked after her children, that she was a widow and there was no good reason for her to stay in Providence, and that if she wanted …

And if she copied them, if she made up her mind instead of merely toying with the idea, if she brought up her old suitcase from the cellar today, if she ran to the station to jump on the first train to anywhere – or to Montreal? Then what? Montreal, sure, a fine place but …

Without even realizing it, she is standing naked on the bathroom tile floor, dripping wet and shivering yet filled with hope. Yes, maybe that is the solution, inside the family though she'd once planted a bomb there.

Above all, she mustn't think. Quickly she dresses and goes down to the cellar for the first time in years.

She's surprised at how little she has: a few clothes, even fewer objects that mattered to her (a small collection of dolls Simon had won at various country fairs and that her daughters, especially Rhéauna, had loved; agates picked up along the shore, their bright veins delighting her; a jewellery box given her by a pink-faced Monsieur Rambert, who claimed that he wanted to fill it over the years to come but that she'd put it away to avoid putting pressure on him). And what about Monsieur Rambert? What to do about him? Let him know – or run away like a thief without seeing him, with no explanation? Without a word about her condition? Don't think about that either; finish packing as fast as she can, leave this damn, unhealthy apartment and ...

Just before she opens the door for the last time, she is overcome by vertigo. It isn't pregnancy nausea, it is uncontrollable terror in the face of the unknown, perfectly ordinary fear about having made the wrong choice and now to be heading forever towards disaster; worry, once again, in the face of unavoidable fate. She has one gloved hand on the doorknob, the other holds her suitcase, and she realizes that what she does in the next few seconds will determine the rest of her life. So it goes. Providence means nothing to her now. Nor do the cotton mills. Or the new university to which, in any case, the child she bears will never have access.

She leaves a note for Monsieur Rambert. She is even weak enough to say where she is going. But without giving her brother's phone number in Montreal. Then again she walks across the city, and, with her little suitcase in hand, she withdraws from the bank the small amount of money she's managed to put aside over the years. Without saying goodbye to her house, her street, her neighbourhood. She's never been happy enough there to feel any regret and she isn't the nostalgic type. On a whim she turns her back on twelve years of her life, without thinking of the consequences. As she'd done when she was twenty. And for once, without "looking elsewhere."

Union Station is enormous. Five buildings! Where to begin? Where to go? It is said to be one of the biggest railway stations in the United States – more than three hundred trains set out every day in all directions – a very important hub for the constantly growing industries of New England. A glorious future was foreseen for Providence and for its inhabitants, the most prosperous and happy of lives built on the ruins of the old station destroyed by fire in 1892, a monstrous monument to the golden age of the industrial era that had started a hundred years earlier. After a quick inquiry of some people who obviously have no desire to help her, Maria finds a man who is kind enough to give her a half-hearted answer: Building Three for trains going north. The ticket seller – a French Canadian whose parents were from the Gaspé – has a good laugh when she asks for the shortest way to Montreal.

"There isn't any shortest way, poor thing. I'm here to tell you, you're in for quite a ride! You'll go through Rhode Island, Massachusetts, New Hampshire, and Maine before you cross into Canada. And even then you won't be there yet! Are you sure you don't want to go just to Boston? The train stops there. And lots of people go there from here to start a new life, they say. Apparently there's tons of jobs. I've got a sister down there. Mind you, it's true she hasn't found a job yet ..."

The first train leaves for Boston in two hours. She buys a sandwich and a local paper and then takes herself over to Platform One, where she settles on a bench, breathing deeply to calm a wave of nausea. The sandwich smells off so she tosses it in the trash and tries to concentrate on the newspaper, but can't.

Then it occurs to her that she is going to arrive in Montreal without a thing: no place to live, no clothes, pregnant, and hidden in the lining of her suitcase enough money saved to keep her for just a few weeks. And on a scrap of paper the phone number of her brother, who may have given her promises without imagining that one day he would have to honour them.

Ridiculous.

She very nearly stands up, tears the ticket, and goes back home to hide out for the next few months, waiting for the birth of the "unwanted" baby she hadn't wanted and who is going to complicate her life. Or should she race over to Madame Bergeron and her torture instruments? Instead Maria stays where she is, hands on her belly, waiting for the train.

Then suddenly, when she least expects it, she raises her head, leans back against the wooden bench, looks at the metal friezes decorating the ceiling – chubby cherubs mingling among the signatories of the American constitution, archangels assailing some poor Indians, an ornamental carved train that runs around the vast room – and starts to laugh. A bracing laugh that starts deep within, that feels good, and that she hopes will take her far.

She picks an old train car that's nearly empty. Only a young man in his twenties occupies one of the two seats that face each other by the window. He is well-groomed and nicely dressed. The boss's son on a business trip most likely or a brand new assistant manager, recent graduate of business school, going to his first serious job. She sits across from him and he greets her politely, then plunges back into his newspaper. He has a long, solemn face, a long, hooked nose, sad eyes and clothes that at first glance are well cut and expensive but, when you look at them more closely, bear the marks of time. The edge of the jacket is threadbare and the trousers are worn at the knees, as if he spent part of his life kneeling in church.

A defrocked priest? Or a visiting Anglican preacher? But those men, she knows, always wear an air of superiority he doesn't possess. What then? A student out on the town who's worn out his trousers from rubbing them under his desk?

She tries to strike up a conversation, something to help her kill time or "look elsewhere" while the train chugs alongside Platform One, leaving the Providence station to take her to an existence of which she knows nothing, which would terrorize her if she gave it any thought. Anything at all could keep her from thinking. He answers in monosyllables, then finally relaxes a little. He even puts his paper down beside him. She's well aware that he thinks she is pretty and she's flattered. When he learns that she's francophone, he switches to French without her having asked. His French is excellent, fluid, somewhat precious, a language that seems to have been learned at school. With a hint of an American accent that she finds charming. She's used to the fat rolled *R*s of the French Canadians in Providence, but the young man's are softer and arrive from the back of his throat like a slight rustling.

He tells her he was born here, in Providence, that he has been a journalist and now hopes to become a writer.

"To write what?"

He seems surprised by her question.

"Novels, Mademoiselle. I'd like to write nice stories. For now I'm devoting myself to poetry but someday I would like to move on to novels ... like many poets."

"What kind of novel?"

He looks at her for a moment before replying. It's as if he's ashamed of what he is going to say.

"It's literature a bit ... special."

She goes pink and lowers her head.

"You mean books people hide to read ... erotic novels? Is that it? Ones we call dirty books?"

His laugh, so unexpected, startles her.

"No, no, nothing like that. That's not what I meant ... They're actually far from erotic ... But let's talk about you ... You were asking me questions just now, but you still haven't said a thing about yourself."

She's on the point of telling him that, till now, her life is far from being an interesting topic of conversation, that her life to date has been merely a series of more or less hopeless misadventures that would bore, not entertain him, even though the journey between Providence and Boston is short, that a budding writer like him would certainly know stories a lot more interesting, in any case not so awkward, when something in his eyes – a glimmer of genuine interest, a new warmth that she hadn't suspected before, a kind of curiosity that was not in the least unhealthy, as is so often the case with priests or pastors, but that springs from sincerity tinged with empathy – stirs in her a sudden urge to confide in someone, to get rid of it all, to shower it all on someone else, even a total stranger who can't do anything to help her. Just offer some relief. He holds out his hand; she only has to let herself be guided.

And it all comes out in one rush, a long, uncontrollable monologue that takes up most of the journey, a flood of words that escape from her with surprising ease. She covers everything: Saskatchewan, her arrival in New England, her marriage, the children she left behind because she had no choice … and her current situation, which she admits to without blushing or lowering her head. She even looks him in the eye while she tells him what she nearly did a few hours before, Madame Bergeron, the broken egg, her disgust and shame at having even thought of it. She expects at any moment to see contempt in his eyes, condemnation by the pastor or the virtuous priest who possesses the truth about everything and who strikes out with an implacable, blind sermon lacking any charity, any indulgence. But no, there's nothing like that. She sees only compassion in the eyes of this man, though he's too young to understand the vagaries of life, to say nothing about helplessness in the face of the ordeals, too great, that fate sometimes has in store.

All the time she speaks, Maria smooths her dress over her thighs as if to get rid of non-existent wrinkles. A little girl's gesture that comes to her when she's embarrassed and doesn't know what to do with her hands. Only the toes of her eyelet boots can be seen under her black skirt, which drags in the sawdust sprinkled on the floor into which the men who smoke pipes spit anytime they want. She'd like to take off her hat, the heat is stifling, but a woman travelling never bares her head or she would pass for someone loose, an adventuress. Yet isn't that what she is, an adventuress, isn't she that in her own way? To leave town with no warning, without telling anyone, to escape a situation that in any case will chase after her no matter where she goes.

The young man doesn't take his eyes off her during the entire confession, delivered in a confidential undertone. She holds his gaze, he dissects her every word but not for a second during the long minutes her story lasts does she feel she is being judged. At church in the dimness of the confessional, she might have broken down in advance of the verbal invective the priest would hurl at her, savouring the humiliation he would inflict on her; but this young man, though she hadn't known him a few hours earlier – a poet on top of it, one of those men with too much imagination, depressive, with such a bad reputation, most of them alcoholic – merely listens while he tries to comprehend her problems instead of judging them. She doesn't expect advice from him, he most likely has no life experience, but she likes having his full attention and the amiability she thinks she can glimpse in his respectful attention.

When she has said everything she has to say, silence falls over the train car again.

The young man frowns, his eyes mist over. It's his turn now to brush some non-existent dust off his trousers. Look at him, more ill at ease than she is.

"Don't you see, it's the only thing I could do? Except kill my child? And go on living the same life with one more reason to feel remorse."

She can see in his eyes that he understands her helplessness and confusion; she also sees that he doesn't know what to say to her, that he would like to cheer her on but doesn't have the words because he's not a woman and men are ignorant of those things, even those men who sympathize and try to understand.

"I know you don't think you can help me. But you already did, just by listening."

He's about to cry like a little boy. Because he is helpless faced with what she has just told him. She is getting ready to console him when the train whistle blows: they are entering the Boston station. Unpleasantly strident noise cuts in two the tenuous thread of understanding that has linked them. And she pities him, a poor, budding writer who hasn't yet found his words and who feels disarmed. Then she smiles at him, and while she is putting on her white string gloves, a little light for the season, thanks him again for listening to her. She even assumes the voice of the women who visited the factory to show their sympathy towards its poor workers:

"What's your name? I'd like to know it in case I see it on the cover of a book – erotic or not."

He gets up, bends down to her, takes her hand, and drops onto it a light, a very light kiss.

"Howard Phillips Lovecraft. And I too am setting out on an adventure of which I cannot predict the outcome, in a city I don't know … I wish you good luck, Madame."

She exits the car without turning around. The next train, in half an hour, will take her a little farther north, she doesn't remember where, in Maine or Vermont.

They don't say goodbye.

She'll never read the magnificent short story entitled "The French Lady on the Train" that will appear a few months later in *The Argosy*, born from a fantastic and macabre vein that will draw attention to him and contribute to launching his literary career.

So this is Montreal?

The train has just turned onto Victoria Bridge, a huge lacy metal structure flung across the renowned St. Lawrence River that Maria has been hearing about all her life – in Saskatchewan because it is the mythic cradle of the French Canadians, and in Providence because people constantly dream of going back there – and that's impressive because of its extraordinary breadth and its colossal grandeur; next to it, the river that cuts Providence in two, beautiful though it is, looks more like a wide spring stream.

She has pressed her nose against the window like a little girl and is trying to guess, just like that, from a distance, a first look, what she knows about the city: yes, there does seem to be a mountain in the middle of the island, but not as high as she would have expected (she'd expected to see something that looked like Vesuvius or Kilimanjaro, photographs of which she'd seen in magazines, but here she is staring at a big brown and grey hill covered with trees that have just lost their leaves – like the New England mountains she'd crossed for the first time the day before, and no higher); the port, buzzing with activity, is huge, but she's not sure it's any more interesting than the one in Providence: lots of very tall buildings but no real skyscrapers; refineries; factories of all kinds, no doubt making a lot of noise; smoke that fills the sky, a sign of considerable industrial activity. It's true then, Montreal is a big city.

And all she has to find her way in this seething, unknown, and maybe threatening place is the phone number of her brother, Ernest, without even an address to find him. What will she do when she gets off the train? Throw herself at the first available telephone? Wait till she has rented a room because she can't turn up at his place unannounced after all? What would he say? And his wife, Alice, whom she's never met and whose existence she was scarcely aware of a few months before? Or board the next train bound for New England because she lacks courage, because she was wrong to leave Providence, because no one here would want her, there's no place for her, her situation won't have changed, and it will take more than a new address to deal with her problems? Especially the one she's facing right now? She brings her hands to her belly.

"Poor baby, I can't lug you around like this much longer. I have to settle down somewhere."

She looks in the direction of the wickets. Men, all middle-aged, advise travellers, sell them tickets for pretty well everywhere in North America. Suitcases, some enormous, are scattered here and there around their owners, heavy and massive, bound in metal or very humble, in boiled leather, tied together with ropes because they're stuffed so full. Maria is well aware that never again would she have the nerve to leave so quickly.

Maria has set her suitcase on the marble floor and walked around and around, her head high, neck craned. This isn't a station, it's a cathedral! The ogival windows, stained glass, arches, archivolt of the ceiling, electric lighting in the middle of the day – it all makes her dizzy. Hundreds of people run all over the waiting room; some jostle her because she's standing in the middle of the traffic, blocking their way; dozens of departures and arrivals are posted on a big metal panel on which the letters change automatically, as if someone or even several people were hidden behind it, replacing the letters as quickly as possible as the schedule changes. In Providence, since the station was scattered over five separate buildings, the waiting room looked like the one in a small provincial station, calm and friendly, but here the arrivals and departures are for all over North America, the ticket window, the boutiques – here the stores are all together in the same place – all make Windsor Station look like a giant beehive.

She feels crushed, insignificant, lost in the aggressive crowd she sees as war-like. Nauseated, she brings her hand to her mouth;

she tries to find the ladies' room. But the wave passes nearly as quickly as it came: nerves, most likely. She picks up her suitcase and then, stepping carefully through the travellers, makes her way towards one of the exits. After all, she's always been resourceful, she can deal with this situation, not react like a little country girl overwhelmed by the big city! She now has a chance to prove it once again and she mustn't allow herself to be intimidated. After all, she can make her way around Montreal without feeling imposed on, can't she? She hasn't exactly come from the backwoods, and she crossed her entire country twelve years earlier so she's seen plenty of train stations.

She spots a woman unwrapping a pile of magazines at a nearby newsstand and approaches her.

"I want to make a phone call. Can you tell me where I might find a pay phone?"

The woman doesn't even raise her head to reply:

"Sorry, I don't speak French."

Her first Montrealer and she doesn't speak French. No way will she speak to the woman in English. She hasn't come all this distance, to the cradle of the Desrosiers, to speak English to the first person she meets!

"Aren't you supposed to speak French in Montreal?"

Finally the woman lifts her head and gives her a sneer that cuts Maria to the quick.

"I told you, I don't speak French!"

A remark emerges from her which she regrets immediately, but it's too late and she realizes that the woman understands perfectly well because suddenly she turns red, as if she'd been slapped:

"*Ah, pis va donc chier!*" Fuck you!

And Maria walks away, head high, to look for a telephone.

DOUBLE FUGUE

MONTREAL

"I hear they had guns hidden in the hold and everything else! If war had been declared that week they'd've killed every single one of us. The whole city of Montreal would've been wiped out!" Teena and Titittle look up from their cards and stare at their sister with disbelief.

"From the port. With just one ship! Come on, Maria, Montreal isn't a village. Anyway, it said in the paper it wasn't true. It was just a rumour. Because the ship was actually German and they didn't know when war would be declared! See if they send guns before it's declared! Honestly!"

"D'you believe everything in the papers?"

"*You* sure did when you read about guns hidden in the hold of a German ship in the port of Montreal a month before the war! Why would that be true and not the opposite? Anyway, war's been declared and nobody's dead!"

"Nobody's dead because there's no German ship in the port."

"What come here are merchant ships, Maria, not warships!

"You never know ..."

"Sometimes, you know, you're really dumb ..."

Teena takes advantage of her two sisters' inattention to swoop down on her ace of spades with a little cry of victory.

"Take a look at this, you dope, stick it under your nose! Game's over! I won!"

Tititte slaps the tabletop, hurts herself with one of her many rings, shakes her hand, making a face.

"You still had an ace?"

Teena wears that superior little look that's so insulting to her two sisters whenever she wins at cards.

"If you hadn't been so busy bickering over a month-old rumour about a German ship that was supposedly loaded with guns, if you'd paid a little more attention to the game, you'd've known the ace of diamonds was still there. We aren't here to talk about warships, we're here to play cards!"

And she picks up the few coins left behind on the table.

Tititte sighs, highly exasperated, and grabs the last soda biscuit spread with Paris Pâté that's sitting in the middle of a white china plate. She bites into the cracker, tears it apart, collects in her palm the crumbs that have fallen onto her chin, and chews with a delighted expression. She loves Paris Pâté – which she actually calls *Pâté de Paris* because it sounds classier – though it's said to be made entirely from ingredients that are bad for the health: it's salty, it's bitter, it almost tastes of fish even though it's supposed to be the liver of something else, beef or pork, she's not sure which. Actually it reminds her a little of London, where that kind of canned food is very popular and of which she has only unpleasant memories. She wipes her hands on her napkin.

"Everybody knows you never feel like playing when you lose. How old are you? Are you about to turn twelve, like your daughter, Nana?"

Maria picks up the empty plate, starts taking it to the kitchen, changes her mind, and turns towards her sister.

"Oh sure, now tell me I'm a poor loser."

"You're a sore loser, Maria Desrosiers, and the night always ends badly if you don't win."

As she does every Monday, her night off, Maria has her two sisters over for what she calls a friendly little game of cards, but that usually ends with vitriolic exchanges because all three – Maria, Teena, and Tititte – are poor losers and the Desrosiers blood that flows in their veins is generally seething.

"As if *you* like losing, Tititte."

Tititte stands and stretches, hands on the small of her back.

"Nobody likes losing, Maria, but not everybody reacts like you do. I hate losing but I don't turn it into a three-act tragedy that never ends and never goes anywhere."

Maria sticks her head in the doorway between the kitchen and the living room, where she has set up the card table she brings out every Monday night.

"You've got a short memory, Tititte. Last week, *you* weren't exactly a pretty sight."

Teena puts her hand up to break in.

"Enough, you two! Don't start over. You've ruined the game, now drop it."

Maria's voice comes a few seconds later.

"More Paris Pâté? There's a bit left in the bottom of the last can. Soda biscuits too."

Tititte sits on the sagging sofa, its hideous colour somewhere between dark brown and anthracite, and that might be mistaken for a sick little animal collapsed and dying in the corner of the room. It's a gift from their brother, Ernest, an old thing his wife, Alice, had wanted to get rid of that had ended up here, in Maria's tiny living room. Maria still can't afford to buy any half-decent furniture and has been forced to accept what her sisters and brother offer, so her apartment that looks like a junk shop shocks Tititte's aesthetic sense. In her opinion, anything attractive in this room came from her.

Tititte thinks for a few seconds, sighs.

"Get on with it. After all, two or three more soda biscuits aren't going to make me fat."

Maria comes back carrying a plate laden with soda biscuits and the rest of the Paris Pâté in its blue metal tin.

"Here, help yourselves. I don't feel like making any more canapés."

Tititte sniggers.

"You call that a canapé? A blob of *Pâté de Paris* on a cracker? First of all, it isn't *Pâté de Paris*, it's Paris Pâté, so stop calling it that; it's getting on my nerves."

Tititte mashes a bit of something soft and greasy onto a flimsy soda biscuit.

"What's wrong with trying to be a little stylish, will you tell me?" Teena's mouth stretches open in a tremendous yawn and she apologizes.

"Who else would try and make Paris Pâté elegant. It isn't stylish, Tititte, it's poor-quality fat they sell cheap to unlucky people who can't afford the real thing. Even my cat turns up his nose at it."

"Your cat's so spoiled he'd turn his nose up at beluga caviar."

"He's no more spoiled than yours, Tititte Desrosiers."

Maria shuts them up with a gesture.

"Time, girls! Time! Let's call a truce, just long enough for me to finish off my sumptuous late-night snack."

With the gestures of a fine lady, Tititte takes another biscuit and spreads a thick layer of fake liver paste.

Tititte thinks she's the most sophisticated of the three Desrosiers sisters because she sells gloves at Ogilvy's, a fancy department store on St. Catherine Street West, where the rich women from Westmount and Outremont do their shopping. The ladies she waits on – men are rare, too taken up by their work to deal with frivolities such as shopping, they have their wives buy their gloves – the women are demanding, snobbish, rude, but Tititte admires their haughty manner, their ruinously expensive clothes, the heavy fragrances they spray on themselves that announce their arrival in fanfares of murdered flowers and that hang around the saleslady for ages after they leave, delicate but insistent. She excuses their arrogance, telling herself that in their place she would do the same. And secretly dreams about it.

Teena is a saleslady too but in a very different establishment. Less chic, much less prestigious too: she sells shoes at L.N. Messier on Mont-Royal Avenue, a store Tititte sees as too cheap for her liking, where she never sets foot: in her opinion the gloves sold there are of poor quality and unworthy of being worn by any self-respecting woman. Actually she shudders at the mere thought that her sister spends her days crouching at the feet of people who take their shoes off in front of her. Teena considers herself lucky for having found this job – for years, she'd been housekeeper in a house at the summit of Mount Royal of which she has a horrifying memory – and she can spend long evenings sharing stories of what is hidden by the not-always-clean long gowns and the rumpled trousers of the inhabitants of the Plateau Mont-Royal. These stories of course don't in the least amuse Tititte, who contents herself with sighing and shrugging when her sisters both burst out laughing.

As for Maria, six nights a week she serves strong drinks in one of those nightclubs on St. Lawrence Boulevard that Mayor Martin has not been able to shut down recently despite an all-out campaign and the support of God-fearing Montrealers. He has even gone so far as to declare: "People don't go to a nightclub to say their prayers!" Tititte read it in *La Presse*. Those disreputable places – Tititte agrees, they are disreputable – stay open despite everyone's knowledge, with their improper cabaret acts often imported from Europe, their reputation for bringing together all the worst of the shady individuals in the city, their scandalous closing hours, not to mention the reputation for debauchery they inflict on Montreal. The year before, Tititte had advised Maria not to accept the job, but her sister told her to get lost, explaining that she needed money if she wanted to see her daughters again. Tititte still thinks Maria was wrong – the return of her eldest, Rhéauna, has been far from a success – and she tries to avoid talking about what Maria has to put up with every night just to survive because it disgusts Tititte a little. She knows it's hypocritical, that Maria may need a compassionate ear, but she leaves that task to Teena, who instead of taking offence, gains from Maria's stories obvious satisfaction – mixed with the giggles of a little girl being taken for the first time out of her naive and childish world ruled by dolls in puffy dresses. Several times Tititte has dropped in on Maria at work and every time she leaves enchanted with what she has seen, as if it were all new to her. Yet there is no lack of experience in her life, for a long time she was reputed to be the wildest of the three Desrosiers sisters, to the point where some of her neighbours – she lives in an apartment on Fullum Street, not far from work – refuse to speak to her. But she'd never dare go to a nightclub on her own, especially not one on St. Lawrence Boulevard, yet every time Maria invites her there she is thrilled and has the time of her life.

33

All three then live without a man in a society where that's not really approved of: Teena has never married despite the many gentlemen who've hung around her – in veiled terms people talk about a child when she was young but that's a taboo subject no one would dare bring up with her; Maria may be a widow but that's not certain; and Tititte, though not divorced because her religion forbids it, came back from London alone, swearing she was fed up with men. These women serve as curiosities in a world governed by men, where women produce a child a year, even in the city where they don't enjoy any independence or freedom.

The evening ends in a forced truce marked by long silences – why talk if you can't argue – that Maria tries as best she can to fill with subjects, all of which fall flat. The card game ended badly and too early for them to leave on the pretext they were going to bed; the snack had been transformed into a judgment of Tititte's culinary taste, the sister who tries to put on haughty airs even when she is eating vulgar Paris Pâté. For a week now nothing special has happened that could restart the conversation, so boredom and embarrassment are settling into the living room of the Montcalm Street apartment, in the heart of a poor, working-class neighbourhood, another source of squabbling between Maria and Tititte actually, because Tititte maintains it's no place to bring up a girl who's almost twelve.

"It was on sale."

Teena and Tititte nearly jump. It's the first time anyone has opened her mouth for a few minutes now and each of them, sipping the strong black tea – in the Desrosiers family it's known as Indian tea – is lost in thought.

Teena sets down her cup.

"What? What was on sale?"

"The Paris Pâté. It was on sale. For seven cents a can instead of ten, at Clavet's on Panet Street. It was worth it."

Tititte clasps her hand over her mouth and gets up, running. "You made me eat pâté you bought for seven cents a can. Are you trying to kill us?"

Teena shoots a look at Maria as if to say, okay enough, let's go. Maria rolls her eyes.

"I'll have you know, Teena Desrosiers, that two minutes ago you thought it was good! Seven cents isn't nothing, you know. And don't talk so loud near the children's room, Théo might wake up. And don't pretend you're sick either, just because I bought it on sale. Honestly! They didn't poison it by dropping the price. You didn't even realize it was cheaper. Which means that it tasted the same as if it had cost ten!"

But Tititte is already in the bathroom making all kinds of unpleasant throat sounds, bringing a smile to her sisters, who are used to these society-lady fits of hers, she who is disgusted by everything and who claims to be shattered by the slightest infringement of the rules of decorum or good taste.

"Tititte! I told you not to wake up the children!"

Too late, Théo has started to howl. Maria crosses the hallway to go and open the door of the bedroom her two children share.

"Rhéauna! Rhéauna! Are you asleep?"

A drowsy voice emerges from under the sheets in the small bed that stands along one of the walls.

"Mmmmh?"

"Théo woke up and I can't take care of him because your aunts are still here."

A head emerges next to her in the doorway. It's Teena, who adores Théo and never misses a chance to pick him up and toss him in the air while covering him with sloppy, blood-red kisses.

"Leave them alone, Teena! They need their sleep."

Rhéauna has pushed off the covers and now sits up while the two women approach Théo's little bed. He wriggles with joy when he spots the silhouette of his mother.

Teena brings her hands to her heart.

"He's so adorable. But he's getting fat. Has he put on weight since last time?"

Maria gently pushes her aside to take her child, who immediately starts to gurgle.

"You can't even see him, Teena, it's too dark!"

Teena is already holding out her arms.

"Let me have him, just for a minute … Come on, Théo, come see Auntie; she's going to bite you till you bleed. Really, he's such an adorable little sweetheart I can't believe it, no sir. I can't. A real baby Jesus."

"Teena, cut it out! You'll get him all worked up again and he'll never get back to sleep when you leave."

"I'll be careful."

"You always say that, but then after you go, you've left me with a bundle of nerves."

Rhéauna is already beside them, ready to look after her little brother.

"How come you woke me up, Mama, if you wanted to look after him yourself?"

Her aunt Teena runs her hand through her hair.

"You've grown up too, Nana. But you haven't got fat. You look like a green onion that grew too fast."

Rhéauna yawns as she pushes away her aunt's hand.

"You say that every time you see me, Aunt Teena, you should try to find something new!"

All three turn their heads towards the door. Tititte has just made her entrance, over her mouth a perfumed handkerchief – a wave of Tulipe Noir quickly fills the room. Maria kisses the baby, then lays him in his cradle.

"Don't makes it worse, Tititte, the bedroom's already too full."

"I want to see him too!"

Maria stands up, arms akimbo.

"Okay, who's in charge here? Get out! Both of you! These children need their sleep. Nana, go back to bed. The rest of you, time to go home."

Rhéauna hadn't slept a wink of course. She had pretended to wake up when her mother burst into the bedroom, though she'd barely gotten into bed. As she did every Monday, the minute Théo was asleep she had moved her little chair to the bedroom door and opened it with tremendous caution, to listen in on her mother and her aunts. Some Mondays, she thinks to herself, she'd have been better off going straight to bed because nothing interesting happened around the card table. Gossip repeated thousands of times about family or the workmates of the three women are exchanged dispassionately. Some totally hare-brained views on fashion or the cost of living are exchanged. (The Desrosiers despair non-stop about the sudden rise in prices and talk a lot about money, which they don't have much of). Diabolical laughter bursts out at the end of funny stories of which the little girl hasn't understood a thing and that always seem to offend aunt Tititte. Well-chosen oaths are levelled, some even by Tititte, before a poorly dealt round of cards.

There are times when Rhéauna falls asleep with her head against the doorpost because what she hears is boring and when she wakes it takes her a few seconds to remember where she is.

Her curiosity is sometimes rewarded, though, by a piece of news they have tried to keep from her and that she's happy to learn, her ear plastered against the half-open door, neck craned, heart beating, a subject they don't want to bring up in front of her because it's intended for adults only. It doesn't have to be anything important; novelty is enough, especially when it's mixed with a slight hint of the forbidden.

And the card game just ending that night proves to be totally fascinating. First of all, rather intriguingly the aunts arrived much later than usual, meaning that for once, what a relief, she was spared the hugs and the cuddles and the compliments she dreads every week because she's sick of hearing the same praise and the same complaints: You're taller, you're pretty now, do you get enough to eat? (aunt Teena). Your mother ought to cut your hair, you look like a gypsy, your dress is too short (aunt Tititte). Tonight her mother had already sent her and Théo to bed when the doorbell rang. She probably thought they were asleep, but Rhéauna heard everything, as usual. And towards the end of the game they raised a topic that has preoccupied Rhéauna for nearly a month now and that made her prick up her ears: the war that has just broken out in Europe.

Unsure at first exactly what that meant (oh, she had an idea of what war was, but for her it was something from the past, from history books, important dates that mustn't be forgotten, it's true, though they were still only dates, a vague and nebulous reality, intangible, they didn't concern her and always happened far away); she'd consulted her old Larousse dictionary and after reading the definition she leafed through *La Presse*, which her mother bought every day and which had devoted a good part of its front page to the subject since war had broken out earlier that month. And there, for the first time, because it was written in that day's paper, because the date was part of her own everyday life and not some far-off and foreign past, the war took on its own horrifying meaning: somewhere, far away over there on the other side of the Atlantic, *right now*, men are fighting, Germans, English, and French in particular, or so she understands; all sorts of instruments of war have been launched, whole cities have been devastated, boats have exploded in the middle of the ocean, and – this is what's tormenting her so much – every day the newspaper prints the question, namely, whether it could cross the ocean and strike here, in North America, in Canada, in Montreal. So when her mother brought up the topic of the German U-boat possibly filled with guns that had been found in the port of Montreal a while back, on the eve of the outbreak of war, her fears came back – the new nightmares she'd been having recently, full of explosions, cries, human flesh torn to shreds, and blood spurting everywhere, the anxious fear that strikes her out of the blue and squeezes her chest in the middle of playing or reading – at the same time as the *idée fixe* that's been haunting her for days and can't get rid of: her mother, her brother, would be safer in Saskatchewan than here. There's no St. Lawrence River in Saskatchewan, not even a good-sized body of water, so warships can't get in; it's empty, it's far away, and nobody is interested.

Rhéauna goes up to her brother's crib, leans over the rail. She can't see him, it's too dark, but she likes to hear him breathe while she tries to make out his motionless little shape, a little paler than the rest of the darkness all around them. At times Théo's breathing is interrupted by sighs or little growls that worried her when she first arrived in Montreal the year before: she thought he was sick, that he was going to die; she panicked, many times she'd had to wake up their mother in the middle of the night. She had realized quickly though, after some tongue-lashings from Maria, that he dreams about angels, that his squirming is normal, that a baby can have nightmares like everyone else. Now she doesn't get upset when she watches him sleep, she lets him squeal, wave his little feet, turn over in his bed with unconscious effort. Sometimes she comes to rescue him, turns him onto his back or belly, pulls up the cover or takes it off if it's too hot. She knows that he guesses her presence, she senses that he is smiling in his disrupted sleep, that he is now holding out his arms to her, his second mother.

She moves her hand, touches his forehead. It's cool. Soft. A knot of emotion rises in her chest, she has trouble swallowing, she knows she shouldn't cry but senses tears are coming, inevitable, that it's pointless to fight them. While she waits she presses her nose against his round little belly. He smells good, of baby powder and a little bit of pee-pee; it smells of life. She starts to hum the melody that Grandma Simone used to sing in their room in Saskatchewan when she and her sisters missed their mother too much or when one of them was too sad: "*Quand nous chanterons le temps des cerises, le doux rossignol, le merle moqueur seront tous en fê-ê-te.*" It's a song with the good smell of new-mown hay, vegetable soup, and coffee perking. The song has the aroma of nostalgia, vague memories that can't be found, an inexpressible lack right there, in the region of the heart, a crushing deprivation they suspect is final, that renders you inconsolable. Before, she was in want of her mother; now ...

Where are they now anyway? Where are they all – Béa, Alice, Grandpa, Grandma? The corn must have finished growing, the haying will begin soon, the silos will be filled with grain, the little country school will open again, Mademoiselle Patenaude will welcome her charges on the front steps, standing straight and proud ... Rhéauna's mother told her that out there in Saskatchewan the sun set two or three hours later than in Montreal, that it was earlier there than here, that they ate their meals long after she did in the east, that in Saskatchewan they were still asleep when she left for school, that they'd just finished supper when she went to bed in Montreal ... Could that be? That the sun doesn't set at the same time everywhere? Or is it an invention of her mother's to keep her from thinking about them too much, from imagining she was doing the same thing they were at the same time, that she's in symbiosis more with them than with her? Rhéauna remembers that Sister Marie-de-l'Incarnation told her she would explain time zones the following year – scissors cut the world into twenty-four different parts, for the twenty-four hours of the day apparently; it's true then, her mother hadn't made it up. There is nothing reassuring about it, though, because she'll have to calculate the time out there whenever she thinks about them.

Ah, the little squeal to show he's hungry; she'll have to make him a bottle. For a while now he hasn't been asking for it so often; but he still cries at night and only a little warm milk will soothe him. She'd better hurry before he wakes their mother. And Rhéauna forgets to cry.

She leaves the room, shuts the door to Maria's bedroom, switches on the kitchen light. Maria has already placed a bottle in a kettle of cold water, just in case ... Rhéauna just has to poke up the fire in the coal stove, it won't be long ...

It's while the water is heating that the sobs come. They arrive long before tears come to her eyes, her mouth starts to quiver. She has to lean against the stove so heavily does it weigh on her heart, like a squeezing hand or a too-heavy stone placed on her chest. It's powerful, it comes from deep within, and it's exhausting.

All that because, recently, she has understood a terrible truth that has thrown her into a near-depression she's still able to hide from her mother but that eventually will become obvious, or she won't be able to stop it from blowing up and *that* won't be a pretty sight – contrary to everything she's been saying over the past year, Maria has no intention of bringing Béa and Alice from Saskatchewan. Not this year anyway. It's already late August, school will start soon; if her sisters were to make the same journey she had, from the village of Maria, Saskatchewan, to Montreal, the trip would already be complete, they would be with her, they'd share Théo's room, the house would be full of their exclamations at the size of the city and it would ring with their stories about what had gone on in the village in the past year. There would be suitcases everywhere, little girls' toys would be all over the house, Théo's laugh would mix with theirs. But nothing is happening. Even if Maria keeps promising they'll be there soon – sounding less and less certain but evasive and secretive – Rhéauna knows perfectly well that it's impossible, it's too late, arrangements haven't been made, she'll still be all alone for at least another year. All alone? No. At least Théo will be there …

She goes back to their room, holding the warm bottle. She switches on the bedside lamp, then leans over the bed again. Théo is awake but he's not crying yet. He does, though, have the look that forecasts floods of tears and the vehement protests of the starving: his forehead is creased, his face red, his little legs squirming, and his hands busy, as if he wants to grab hold of everything around him, anything at all – his doggies, the bars of his crib, the blankets – and gobble it up.

"Stop screeching, I'm coming … Look at the nice bottle … Yum-yum! Doesn't that look good!"

He looks at her with his big brown eyes, smiles when he sees the bottle, holds out his arms.

"You're the biggest little piggy I've ever seen. What's got into you? You were sleeping through the night, we finally had some peace and quiet …"

She watches him suck while she holds the bottle. He squeaks with pleasure while he sucks up the milk to which she has added a little maple syrup, just a little, to make it taste better. He flexes his legs, plays with his toes, releases a little fart that drives his sister away from his bed for a few seconds.

"And now I have to change your diaper too … Your potty's already bought, it's at the back of the closet and, believe me, I can't wait to show you how to use it … But I guess it isn't time yet, you're still too young to do it right."

She rests her chin on the edge of the crib, runs her hand through his hair. He's a big baby but many of the details are tiny: his hands, his feet – it's as if they don't change while the rest is growing almost before her eyes – his nose is not at all like the Desrosiers, whose proboscis, according to family trait, is significant – Uncle Ernest is the best example – instead Théo's nose is something slight and turned up, comical, that she likes to squeeze between her thumb and forefinger. And the beautiful mouth, neatly drawn and strawberry red. But so small you wonder how such huge screams can come out of it.

"Wouldn't you like to go and live in the middle of a great big cornfield, with *three* big sisters, a grandpa, a grandma, animals, a white house that always smells of something delicious cooking? A mother too, if she wants to follow us … We'd buy you a dog named Prince, or Blackie, and he'd be the love of your life for a while. He would be the one practically to raise you. Even if the whole world blows up – the French and the Germans have been cutting each other's throats for years – we'd be fine, safe from it all because the war couldn't make it all the way here."

His bottle now empty, he sucks anyway; she takes it away so he won't swallow too much air. He's drunk on milk and he can't protest.

"That's it, all gone, no more till tomorrow. Now make your little burp and go to sleep."

She picks him up, presses him against her shoulder, pats his back. "And don't arrange to be sick on my new nightie."

She hears a kind of hiccup followed by a sensation of dampness and warmth on her shoulder.

"I guess I don't need to bother asking, do I?"

There is a sour little smell that she hasn't yet got used to. Wrinkling her nose, she puts her brother back in his bed, puts on a clean nightgown, and goes back to bed.

Her dreams that night are about spectacular explosions in red and black, entire panoramas that burst with a deafening sound of thunder, combined with visions of bucolic landscapes depicting endless prairies of golden wheat with a kindly wind caressing four individuals, two old people, two children, who wave to her and call her by name. Billows of smothering black smoke are followed by fields of gently undulating wheat, bouts of infernal noise by swathes of perfect calm. She fidgets for hours, pushes away the blankets when she's hot, pulls them back up when she's cold, moans, lets out cries of distress that wake her brother and make him cry, but she hears nothing, she is absent from all reality, lost in a terrifying bloody battle somewhere across the ocean or drowned in a cornfield in another part of the country that's too quiet not to be suspect. This switching from noise to quiet, from aggressive lights to soft sparkling, exhausts her and when she wakes at dawn she feels as if she's run a thousand miles.

While she is fixing her little brother's porridge at about seven o'clock she makes a serious decision. After the dreams, so powerful she's still trembling, she is convinced that it's her duty to save them from the war – her mother, Théo – to take them away from it. After all, if Maria hasn't brought her other two daughters here, it may be to keep them safe from the danger threatening them, but she lacks the courage to leave Montreal herself because she makes a good living here … How much would it cost for three train tickets to Saskatchewan? How much has she put aside in her piggy bank? Enough? No? She'll go get it right after breakfast and while her mother is still asleep she'll break her bank, count how much she has, and ... and what? How could she find out? What to do?

Cross the city. That's it. Take her money and go west along Dorchester because she knows that's where she'll find Windsor Station. Go to the ticket office and buy three tickets for Saskatoon. Faced with a *fait accompli*, her mother will have to go along with it and they'll be safe from the war.

When her mother gets up, a little too early unfortunately, and makes her way to the bathroom for some Aspirin – she and her sisters had overdone the Bols gin the night before, and Maria wonders if Teena and Tititte will be able to get to work if their headaches are as bad as hers – Rhéauna asks permission to go out for a few hours. She'd like to go to Dupuis Frères for school supplies. It's not very far, there's no risk of her getting lost. She can go by herself now, she's old enough and, this year, she would like to buy pencils and scribblers without Maria's intervention. Her mother's head hurts too much to argue so she agrees, telling Rhéauna that she still has to be home by noon. Rhéauna says she'll be home long before then, that she'll even make lunch while Maria recovers from her card game; then Rhéauna races to her bedroom, leaving her brother with his bowl of porridge.

She has to figure out how to break her china piggy bank without making too much noise. Which won't be easy. She could insert a knife into the slit in the top to try and make some coins fall out one by one but that would take hours and she has no time to waste.

She picks up her bank, turns it over and over. It was a birthday present from her aunt Teena, almost as soon as she'd arrived in Montreal the year before, with the suggestion that she should try filling it for a whole year so she can buy herself something nice on September 2, 1914, the day she turns twelve. The piggy bank is very ugly but she didn't dare say so when she opened the gift. Pink and blue, a stupid smile, and a corkscrew tail. Every time she was able she dropped in a coin, telling herself that her next birthday party would be sensational, with lots of candies, paper flutes, streamers, all paid for by her.

She smiles. Who knows, maybe her birthday party will be held at her grandparents; her sisters would be delirious and there would be an enormous cake, the one her grandmother calls a 1-2-3-4 cake that tastes so deliciously of vanilla and that would take three or four days to eat ... No. She sits on her bed. She knows it's ridiculous, that it's an impossible dream, that she can't force her mother to pull up stakes and move just because Rhéauna's afraid of the war. And her piggy bank probably doesn't have enough money for even one train ticket. But is that really why she's getting ready to break her china piggy bank, is fear of war the real reason she wants to run away?

She goes back to the kitchen for Théo, who is in his high chair playing with what's left of his oatmeal, now dried out in the bowl, flinging bits on the floor, squealing happily. He has some in his hair and, beaming and excited, he doesn't seem to mind it too much. Cleaning him off with a damp cloth – he howls and kicks, he hates having his face washed and wishes he could go on playing the new game he's just invented – she remembers there's a hammer in a drawer of the kitchen cupboard. She can't think of any other way to break her piggy bank but wonders how she'll do it without waking her mother ... She finds the hammer almost at once in the top drawer and comes back to their room, Théo still howling and squirming in her arms.

"If you don't wake up Mama with your yelling, for sure a little hammer will do it."

But her mother's voice comes to her from Maria's bed:

"If you don't shut that kid up right now, Nana, I'll strangle him myself!"

"I'm changing his diaper, Mama, he'll stop in a minute ..."

She sits her little brother on the floor next to her bed.

"Watch this. Nana's going to break her piggy bank and it will make a noise ... You'll love it, you'll see ..."

It's as if he understands because he stops crying and, with snot running from his nose, gawks at her.

"Noise – that's fun, isn't it? You're right, for once we're allowed to make a noise, let's enjoy it ... And meanwhile you should start howling while I use the hammer; Mama won't punish me, her head hurts too much."

She leaves the china piggy bank on her pillow, and gets an idea. She moves the bank onto the carpet, covers it with the pillow, then grabs the hammer.

"Maybe you don't know this, Théo, but I'm going to do something really, really important."

One well-aimed blow and the piggy bank explodes under the pillow. There's a rather disappointing little thud. Théo keeps looking at his sister as if he's wondering when he's going to hear the promised noise.

She lifts the pillow. Coins, lots of coins, are mixed in with the pink-and-blue china debris. It's hard to imagine that it once looked like an animal. The ears maybe, or the corkscrew tail or the snout which is intact. She pushes away the sharp broken pieces, picks up the coins. Five, ten, and twenty-five cent pieces but not one big silver dollar. She just received one, for Christmas, and quickly spent it without even thinking of putting it in her piggy bank.

"Gosh, I've got way more than I thought!"

Exactly seven dollars and eleven cents. For her it's a sizable amount, she's never had so much money in her possession, but she doesn't know if it's enough for three one-way tickets to Saskatchewan. She suspects it's not, that her plan is ridiculous and doomed to fail, but seven dollars and eleven cents isn't nothing, it could take them far!

Then suddenly she faces facts: she didn't really intend to buy a train ticket for her mother. Because Maria would never agree to leave? Maybe. But even more because she'd like to go away by herself, with Théo. To run away with him to the other end of the world. To find again her lost paradise. Without their mother, who in any case could never be happy there because of bad memories that she holds on to and that surface sometimes in sudden shouts when she's had too much to drink. Rhéauna is not ashamed of herself; she doesn't think she's heartless or ungrateful, she's just making an observation that, while it puzzles her, doesn't make her feel the least bit guilty. Maria will understand. That it's for the good of everyone. All three. Or not. She will buy three tickets, she'll hide them and, tomorrow, or the day after … She doesn't want to think any further, she knows it would discourage her. What verb would she use to say that the very scope of the plan would keep her from moving. And she needs to move, to try at least, to do something so she can go back there, go back home.

She picks up Théo.

"I'm going to put you down in Mama's bed, Théo. You know how much she loves that … I'll leave you with a nice bottle and then you'll go to sleep. Okay?"

🍍

Rhéauna puts on her red cotton dress that's a bit too short because she's grown a lot over the summer but in which she still thinks she looks pretty. Who knows, maybe it's the last time she will wear it. Then she takes out her patent-leather shoes for Sunday and puts the seven dollars and eleven cents in her change purse, which she stows in a bag with a long strap she'll wear over her shoulder. For once it contains something more than a clean hanky and a few pennies.

All right, good, let's go. Rhéauna is ready.

Before she leaves her room she looks at herself in the little mirror above her toy chest.

Ready for the great adventure? Ready for the great adventure.

She knows that's not true. That she doesn't really know what she's embarking on. All the same, she leaves her bedroom with the resolute steps of someone who's sure of what she is doing and is convinced that she's right.

Her mother's voice, again.

"You leaving already?"

Rhéauna opens Maria's bedroom door.

"Sure."

"It's way too early. The stores won't be open yet, for heaven's sake, it isn't even nine o'clock!"

"I'll wait at the door."

"You know I don't like it when you walk outside by yourself …"

"There's no danger, Mama, I'll go along St. Catherine Street. It's just a few blocks from here … I'll walk slowly and when I get to Dupuis Frères it will be open. I promise I won't take my money out of my purse unless I find something to buy … And it will just be things for school."

Théo is crying beside Maria, who puts her hand on his belly.

"I hope he didn't eat too much porridge, sometimes he has trouble digesting it."

She leans over, drops a kiss on his forehead.

"Isn't he an adorable baby! Just look at the cuddly little boy …"

Rhéauna's heart melts in her chest at the affection her mother shows to her little brother.

She doesn't have the right to separate them.

She'll persuade her mother to follow them, that's all. After she buys the darn train tickets of course.

Don't think any further. Act. Hurry up, don't think, get a move on …

"I'll be back for lunch … Way before, even …"

"I hope you are, or you'll be sorry."

Descending the spiral staircase that goes from the outside balcony to the brand new concrete sidewalk, Rhéauna thinks about Little Red Riding Hood and smiles. She's on her way into the unknown too but it's not a forest that she will cross, it's a city, and it's not a basket of provisions she'll take to her grandmother, it's a grandson!

"Which station?"

"Windsor."

"Windsor Station in Montreal?"

"That's right."

"Why there?"

"I got off a train, what d'you think?"

"You just arrived in Montreal?"

"There's a good chance that's what I mean." Maria had hesitated before dialling the number, now she regrets it. She's never been close to her brother, Ernest, and the twelve years they've just spent apart won't sort matters out between them. He was arrogant when he was young, probably still is. As is she, for that matter.

"What're you doing in Montreal? Are you on vacation?"

"You think I can afford a vacation? I was working in a cotton mill if you recall, Ernest, my vacation I spent at home reading stupid novels because I couldn't afford anything more interesting!"

"What're you doing here anyway?"

One thing is clear: the voice isn't as friendly as when she had called him from Providence. She doesn't feel any warmth, any friendliness; this time it's a chill that prevails. He may already have guessed why she called and is getting ready to hang up on her. No, he won't go that far. Not to the sister he hasn't seen for so long.

"I've left Providence for good."

"Just like that, all of a sudden."

"Hardly, I'd been thinking about it for a while."

"You could've let us know before you got on the train to Montreal ... Why the big surprise? Turning up without telling anybody first ..."

She feels like saying point blank why she left Providence, that she herself didn't know the day before that she was going to leave, but she holds back. She has to prepare him, not pour it out all at once, poor man, especially not on the telephone.

"Look, Ernest, I've just spent hours and hours on trains going in every direction, now and then getting vaguely closer to Montreal. I crossed through I don't know how many states, anyways a good part of New England, I ate badly, I hardly slept, I felt sick, I'm beat, I can't feel my butt or my back, this is no time for a sermon ..."

"I'm not preaching a sermon ..."

"No, but I can feel it coming ..."

"Listen, Maria, how come you're calling me? You didn't phone just to tell me not to preach a sermon!"

Still the same bad faith in an argument, he's like that every time. Steer the conversation to another subject to avoid the real one. She'd like to tell him to piss off, then hang up before he does.

"When you called me in Providence you said that if I needed help ..."

He cuts her off before she finishes the sentence.

"So on top of everything else you need help?"

"It's scary how glad you are to hear me."

So now she's using the same strategy he uses.

"I didn't say I wasn't glad to hear you but I never imagined I'd hear you call from Windsor Station, that's all. From the backwoods of Rhode Island where you hid out centuries ago, maybe, but not from a station in Montreal! If you'd told me you were coming I'd've waited for you at the station, you wouldn't have had to call me, you must understand that ..."

"That's kind of why I phoned you, actually ... Could you come and pick me up?"

"Pick you up? What do you mean? I haven't got a car and I'm not a millionaire either. Pick you up and take you where? You surely don't want to sleep here?"

She doesn't answer. Maybe he understood as he was saying it that was what she was counting on. She can almost hear him think.

"Maria? Are you still there?"

"Where else would I be? Listen ... Just tonight ... I'd need to stay at your place just tonight, long enough to rest for a while and then tomorrow I'll go and rent a room somewhere before I start looking for a job."

She hears a woman's voice behind him, speaking English. Her sister-in-law, Alice, most likely, whom she's never known because Ernest met her in Winnipeg when Maria had already settled in Providence.

"Is that your wife I hear?"

"Yes. She wants to know who's calling at this time of night."

"It's not that late."

"It is for *her*."

"She goes to bed with the chickens?"

"No. To her, hens go to bed late."

They both laugh. It's the beginning of complicity. Now she has to take advantage of it.

"Explain to her that your sister Maria, from Rhode Island, has just arrived in Montreal. She must know I exist, doesn't she?"

"You exist, sure, but I'm not sure that would help you."

"Because of what you've told her about me?"

"Me and our two sisters, yes."

"You aren't embarrassed?"

"Look, Maria, have you ever given us even one reason to say something good about you? And I can't see why we're talking about it on the phone."

"That's right, we could explain better in person."

"Don't try, Maria, I remember you're a troublemaker."

Their complicity was of short duration.

His wife's voice again. He tells her in English to shut up. In a tone that reminds Maria of the insolent young man who gave himself the right to behave idiotically because he went to Mountie school. A tremendous hunk of a man, lingering in adolescence, who realizes he has a cumbersome body, but is unaware of his strength, who could become dangerous when overly contradicted. The way he treats his wife suggests that he is still the same, pretentious and superior, and that the affection shown to his sister on the phone some months earlier may have been simply a momentary weakness. Just the policeman in him, finally, the explorer of archives, the shuffler of papers, who was glad he'd found a trace of her after years of searching.

"I told her. I can't say she's thrilled to see you here."

"I understand English, Ernest, I've just come from the United States. And she didn't say a word, you have no idea what she thinks."

"And you have no idea how she looks ..."

Nothing is more embarrassing than silence on the telephone. And this silence was stretching out dangerously. The positions are clear, Maria has imagined things and Ernest has made a decision that is final, permanent, irrevocable.

Maria takes a big gulp of air.

"Okay, listen. I'm sorry I thought my own brother'd be glad to see me after all these years."

"No blackmail, Maria, that won't work ..."

"What am I supposed to do, hang up because you couldn't care less about me?"

Alice's voice again, tiny, docile. Of course, it is to be expected, her husband has married a submissive woman, a mouse who has never made a decision in her life, who depends on him to live and breathe and who goes to bed before the hens.

"Listen, Maria, Alice says it's okay. For tonight. She says we can't just leave you out on the street all alone."

Her opinion of her sister-in-law changes in a quarter of a second. What a marvellous woman! She feels like laughing at her own hypocritical turnabout.

"Okay fine, I won't get in your way. I'll sleep wherever I can. Where d'you live?"

"A good ways away, Ville-Émard. Take the streetcar, the *p'tits chars*."

"The what?"

"*P'tits chars*. A streetcar ... Look, take the St. Catherine streetcar going west all the way to the end, Atwater Street, and I'll pick you up."

"You haven't got a car."

"We'll take a taxi."

"I can't afford taxis, Ernest!"

"Do as I say and quit arguing! Jesus! You haven't changed, eh, you're still the same, you always have to put in your two cents' worth so you'll get the last word."

"My God, Ernest, I only said I can't afford a taxi. You haven't changed either, have you? You don't have to, you know. I'm not asking you to take me all over town in a cab. I'll rent a room, wait till tomorrow to get together, we can even not see each other at all if that's what you want!"

So they're off, both worn out. In the past it could go on for hours and more than once it ended badly.

"Maria, you asked for help so take it now and quit arguing. You just have to go up Windsor Street to St. Catherine, then you take the streetcar heading west, there's nothing to it. How big is your suitcase?"

"I'm all right, I didn't bring much."

"Okay fine, I'll be at the Atwater Station in half, three-quarters of an hour … Tell me what you look like anyway so I'll recognize you."

"You'll see when you see me, fat pig!"

"How come you know that I'm fat?"

"All the Desrosiers men are heavy, I don't see why you'd be an exception. Unless they automatically put you on a diet in the Mounted Police so you'll be even more handsome in your beautiful red uniform."

He hangs up without adding a word.

She's had the last word again. A piddling reward.

Now she's upset by the gloom that falls over her. She rests her forehead against the phone and tries to breathe deeply. She wishes she could die right there, in the middle of Windsor Station. What lies ahead, what she hasn't allowed herself to think about since the day before, is too enormous, as she now realizes. After all, she's too smart to have made such a crazy decision, isn't she? She's never been a dreamer, always tries to stay in control of whatever could happen to her, despite her impulsive behaviour. So why this hasty departure, this uncharacteristic flight in the face of a problem, the solution to which certainly won't be found here in Montreal? No, the only solution would probably be to reboard the train for Providence, go back to her job, claiming some fleeting illness, go and see Madame Bergeron with her damn knitting needles, to have an abortion without telling Monsieur Rambert. No.

No.

Keep not thinking, even if it's unlike her. Let herself go. Let life follow its course. No, that's also too stupid. What then? Where will she give birth to this child, under what circumstances, with what money?

She rushes to the ladies' room and vomits copiously, then she leaves the station.

As soon as she leaves the crowded, noisy station, Maria realizes that Windsor Street is quite peaceful. Victorian houses with pointed roofs and cornices of all kinds are partly hidden by magnificent, ancient trees that have already shed most of their leaves. Fall is more advanced here than in Providence and she feels obliged to put on her coat again, pulling up the collar because of the wind – dry, chilly, insistent.

Her suitcase isn't too heavy, she has no trouble carrying it. Still it's strange not to have accumulated more in twelve years; that is, more essential items she didn't want to leave behind. A few dressy dresses; a single hat, the one she wears now; a cedar chest – not Monsieur Rambert's, it's too cumbersome – filled with costume jewellery not worth much but that she finds pretty and flattering. Underwear because you can't go without it. Several pairs of gloves, evidence, in the bourgeois town of Providence anyway, that they are dealing with a real lady. A single perfume, a large bottle of lime-blossom eau de toilette, inexpensive but not strong, that she's worn for years and worries she won't be able to find in Montreal. Her other belongings – furniture, most of it wobbly and bought cheap; shabby rugs; reproductions hung up more to dress the walls or conceal the hideous wallpaper than to try and decorate; all the cushions gleaned here and there over the years according to her needs, piled up chaotically, sometimes forgotten in their corner, things she hadn't recognized when she came home the day before; she'd taken nothing and had no regrets. Without even locking the door she left like a burglar, with no note for the landlord; she'd always considered him to be a real thief anyway. She was repeating what she'd done twelve years earlier, when she'd left her village after a falling-out with her family, resentment in her belly, confusing her tracks so they would never find her, thinking she was free. She had left Saskatchewan in search of freedom and it was slavery she found. Just yesterday she'd thought she was leaving all that behind but what will she fall into now? Especially in her current state? Do sudden impulses always end up costing too much?

It's a beautiful evening, with the scent of fallen leaves that she kicks aside to clear a path, and the recent rain that hasn't had time to dry. Someone at the station had explained that she was headed to the western part of the city, the richest one, that she'll be just off St. Catherine Street; she won't have to wait very long because these little cars come frequently. She smiles in spite of herself. What an odd expression. If there are *p'tits chars* there must be big ones too. And what would big cars be? Streetcars? Are there small streetcars and big ones? She tells herself that she'll have to get used to the way they speak French here after she'd had to cope with the New England variety that's so different from her own. But according to what she's heard from her brother, the difference between Montreal and Providence is not as great as that between Saskatchewan and New England. There are more French Canadians from the east who've settled in New England than the rare westerners like her. And after all, French is still French however it's pronounced.

She crosses Dorchester, a wide and brightly lit street; a passerby, a corpulent woman with a genuine French-from-France accent, a little like that of her in-laws, tell her that St. Catherine is the next street to the north and that she can't miss it.

She walks past a fabulous hotel, the Windsor, across from a big park, deserted at this hour of the day. She imagines that just one night at the Windsor would cost a good part of her fortune, dreams for a moment of doing something wild, finally shrugs and smiles. Still, she stops in front of the main entrance, cranes her neck to try and see inside, eventually goes away under the strict gaze of the doorman, who judges her by her haggard look and her cardboard suitcase.

She's heard a lot about *la Catherine* – as Montrealers call her – from newcomers she worked with over the years who described it as the eighth wonder of the world. (People in the city of Quebec spoke in the same way about rue Saint-Jean.) St. Catherine is the main shopping street in Montreal, lively, deafening, the traffic apparently impossible, a mix of coaches, cabriolets, streetcars, horses and buggies, automobiles; you can find everything there, even fruits and vegetables that don't grow in Canada because of winter. At prohibitive prices, of course. Oranges. Bananas. Lemons. Pineapples. A distant memory: "Have you ever eaten a pineapple, Madame Rathier? They say it's out of this world. And expensive." Everything looks pretty, just as they said it would. Maria is impatient to check everything on the spot – maybe she'll see a pineapple in a display window, she'd never thought about looking for one in Providence – and increases her pace. Lights glimmer straight ahead, she's nearly there.

When she arrives at the intersection with St. Catherine Street she's a little disappointed. There's a lot of light, it's true, traffic is dense, there's a good smell of horse manure that an old gentleman is picking up with a shovel and a bucket, tacking among the coaches with their capering horses and the cars that are honking

their horns – the sidewalks, all concrete, are impressively broad –
but she had expected something more exciting, a kind of perpetual
Christmas Eve, the mythic thoroughfare, the heart of Montreal,
its Champs Élysées. The street is not as broad as she would have
thought, not so noisy; the store windows aren't all lit up; finally, it's
a kind of provincial hubbub not all that different from what is heard
on the commercial streets of Providence. But Montreal is Canada's
metropolis, its biggest port, the most thriving industrial city. The
second French city in the world, or so they say. She deserves a
more imposing downtown than this, doesn't she? Maria may be too
tired to see all of it, after all, to record all that is beautiful, unique
before her eyes. She was overly ambitious and, as usual, she finds
herself facing a truncated version of her dreams. The story of her
life, a condensed version of what always happens to her, every time.

She puts down her suitcase. Now then, which way is west? And
where do you board the streetcar? Does she have to hail it or does
she wait at a street corner? She asks a hurried young man who looks
at her as if she'd emerged from a hole in the sidewalk – until he
notices her suitcase.

"Just arrived?" He has called her *tu*.

She would like to slap him. It's the first time a total stranger has
said such a thing right on the street. Are all Montrealers this rude?

He explains, though, very politely and in detail how and where
to catch the streetcar. She supposes she'll have to get used to this
too – everyone in the city saying *tu* to everyone else and it's not
seen as bad manners.

"Where from? For a holiday or for good?"

She is already crossing the street, suitcase in hand. A taxi offers
to pick her up, she replies that she's going too far; the driver asks
where, she tells him Ville-Émard; he turns his head away, the
car picks up speed, disappears into the traffic. Okay, now what?
Is Ville-Émard a disreputable neighbourhood where even the most
hardened taxi drivers refuse to go? Just what she needs ...

An enormous contraption in green and yellow metal approaches,
spitting sparks. At last, something bigger than in Providence, where

the streetcars are tiny. This one is gigantic, threatening, it makes a hell of a noise when it brakes, like a big train car moving along on its own, without an engine. The door creaks open, a wrought-iron running board greets her. The driver leans in her direction.

"Your suitcase is too big! Get in at the back."

Get in at the back? Oh right, there's another door at the back of the machine. She runs, sets foot on the step, places her suitcase next to a fat man with a braid-trimmed cap who sits enthroned in a kind of polished-wood cabin, like a pulpit in church. He smiles at her.

"You just got in at Windsor Station. I guess you don't know what it costs?"

Before he even finishes his question she realizes that she doesn't have any Canadian money. She forgot – actually she didn't take the time – to change her U.S. money before leaving Providence. She doesn't listen to the price he tells her but leans against the ticket-taker's stand, disheartened.

"You'll think I'm crazy but I haven't got any Canadian money. I forgot. I wasn't thinking. I know it's crazy but I didn't think."

He looks hard at her, frowning.

"You haven't got Canadian money or you haven't got any money, period?"

She startles, cut to the quick.

"I've got money!"

She opens her handbag, takes out her change purse.

"Here. I've got tons. But as you can see, it's American money."

He sighs, tears off a ticket, hands it to her.

"Give me five cents and we'll be even."

She suspects it's too much but she has no choice, sits on one of the threadbare benches of woven straw that over time has taken on an ugly brownish hue.

It's an old open streetcar; Maria has to pull up her coat collar to cover her neck and ears. What must it be like in the dead of winter! But maybe these contraptions are used only during warm weather, maybe when the winter cold arrives they're replaced by closed and, let's hope, heated streetcars. She thinks to herself that it's time to take out of circulation these piles of rusty old iron that advance along rails made shiny by wear. Maybe during the winter that's soon to arrive they will go into hiding in some garage or other. Meanwhile, everyone is freezing.

The few passengers, muffled up in their coats like her, keep looking down at their knees. No one is reading, no one is looking outside. The sightseeing here, though, is interesting. Maria finally lets herself admire the department stores – she passes the stunning windows of Ogilvy's, where she does not yet know that her sister Tititte works – and gazes at the unbelievable diversity in the means of transport that congest St. Catherine Street. They move, they shriek. Not only are there horse buns, the smell of which she quickly recognizes when the streetcar turns off Windsor Street, but it also smells of engine exhaust because there are a lot more cars here than in Providence. A smell, unpleasant and pungent, makes her take a handkerchief from her purse. As she is blowing her nose, she notices that the women around her aren't wearing gloves. She is nearly shocked. After all, these women, apparently coming home from work and whose company she might soon keep, may not be able to afford gloves to wear outside. She thinks again about winter. What do they do in the winter? What will *she* do, with her little white string gloves? She looks towards the suitcase she's left beside the ticket seller. Had she thought about packing wool gloves? Probably not.

The streetcar jolts, squeals, stops.

The driver gets up from his seat and stretches, both hands on his lower back.

"Terminus! All change!"

Already! Maria thought she was going much farther into the interior of the island of Montreal. She glances outside. This square lined with young trees is too tiny to be considered a real park. The other passengers get out; she will let them all leave while she keeps an eye on her suitcase. When she's alone she rises, grabs her case.

"I hope you know where you're going. It's getting late."

She sets her suitcase on the running board.

"Okay, yes. My brother's supposed to be waiting for me here."

"Do you see him?"

"I haven't looked."

"Maybe he isn't here yet ..."

"Maybe."

"Too bad we have to turn the streetcar and set off right away, otherwise I'd have offered to wait with you."

Before she gets out – without a single glance at him – she thanks him for keeping an eye on her suitcase. Most important, don't give him reason to hope.

"A pretty girl like you, mustn't let her get away!"

He's in a bad way, poor guy; she feels anything but pretty after the long train trip ... Another sneaky one in the big city who can't spot a woman in his field of vision – regardless of what she looks like – without coming on to her. He must lay on tons of compliments in the course of a day spent racing from one end of St. Catherine Street to the other. She knew braggarts like him at the mill, petty bosses who took advantage of their petty powers, a race of despicable men she would brush aside with a flip of her hand once their compliments and innuendo were done. This time, though, she can't keep from smiling and she places her gloved hand over her mouth.

Then, something unbelievable happens. Just as she steps onto the sidewalk in search of a bench where she can wait for Ernest, the streetcar turns around! She's never seen anything like it. In Providence she lived at one end of a streetcar line and never wondered how they reversed direction ... But here, after searching around in the rails, more numerous here than elsewhere, using a long metal pole, the driver and the ticket seller push, cursing and sweating, on the front of the vehicle. It starts to turn on a worm-eaten wooden plate that creaks and moans. When they have finished, they look in her direction, no doubt to check whether she has admired their strongman act. The ticket seller waves at her briefly, then bows slightly.

"Takes muscles to be a streetcar conductor you know! If you need a real man ..."

They burst out laughing as they reinstall the streetcar's cogwheel on the wire stretched out above it. Sparks shoot out just as the wheel touches the electrical wire and Maria thinks about how it had frightened her the first few times she rode the streetcar, originally down in Boston, then in Providence.

The two men get back in the machine and wave at her as they head back into the city, following the line from one end to the other. They are familiar but polite. At least she's found that out about Montrealers tonight … In any case, they didn't call her *tu* like the arrogant young man a while ago.

She looks around. The small square is empty. She's in the middle of nowhere, in the cold, at the end of the streetcar line, in a strange city, waiting for a brother she probably won't recognize, who may treat her like a foreigner. What a wonderful trip!

Has Ernest also come by streetcar to save money? After all, he must make a good salary in the RCMP. Unless paper-pushers aren't treated as well as the valiant soldiers in red, pride of the Canadian west riding high on their prancing horses. The fact is that she's in eastern Canada now, isn't she? What are the Mounties doing here? She thought it was a "phenomenon" of the western provinces.

She wonders if she'll wait for long. Is Ville-Émard very far away? First of all, is it a town outside Montreal or an isolated neighbourhood? She is about to settle on a wooden bench – hoping she won't fall asleep – when a taxi pulls up with impressive backfiring and a cloud of smoke that makes her nauseous. She turns, leans forward: is she going to be reunited with her brother after all these years? A few seconds go by. Someone is looking at her through the open window. Then the door opens.

No. The man who gets out of the car, massive, awkward, breathless even though he hasn't really exerted himself physically in the minutes before, is nothing like the vigorous country boy she left behind in Saskatchewan, of whom it was said he'd most likely become a lumberjack if he lived anywhere but the prairies where there are no trees to fell. He is squeezed into the overcoat of a serious man, shapeless, colourless, too small for him, head crushed into a stiff, broad-brimmed hat reminiscent of the one he must wear with pride when he's in his Mounted Police outfit. A pathetic reminder of the powerful uniform that here is more of a loser's costume. When he straightens up – he's a good head taller than she is – it's by his mug that she recognizes him. Everything about him has changed except the nose – huge, red, scarred with teenage acne, the flaw their father called the curse of the male Desrosiers because only the men in the family were afflicted, but Ernest was proud because of the claim that a big nose heralded the respectable size of another anatomical protuberance. (He talked about it all the time, in veiled terms so as not to make his mother's and sisters' faces get too red. In any case, the girls acted as if they didn't understand, so much so that their friends were calling him Ernest-with-the-big-prick, though they'd never seen it.) His cheeks, streaked with red veins since his teens, were puffy, there were bags under his eyes, wrinkles lined his forehead, but his nose was unchanged. The shape anyway, because it too had gotten quite red over the years. Alcohol? Goddamn alcohol, another scourge of the Desrosiers men!

"Maria?"

"Ernest?"

The seconds that follow are painful. What should they do? Throw themselves in each other's arms? Why? Neither of them missed the other. Shake hands? That would be ridiculous. After all, they're not strangers. They are content to look at each other.

Finally Ernest bends over and picks up her suitcase.

"I thought you'd've changed a lot more."

"Never mind, it's okay, I know I'm fat."

"You aren't just fat ..."

He interrupts her: you might think he was about to dump the suitcase on the sidewalk and run away.

"I'm old? Is that what you want to say, I'm old? I'm not all that old, I'm barely forty!"

For sure she isn't going to say that he looks fifty.

"That's not what I meant either. We've both aged, Ernest, it's normal. I'm sorry but we're off to a bad start ... We haven't seen each other for years, this is no time for squabbling."

"What were you trying to say anyway?"

"Nothing. Nothing. I just wanted to answer you and say something."

"That's what I told you just now ... You still always want the last word."

"Right, I do."

"See, you just did it again."

"Did what?"

"You talk back when I say something ... to get the last word! To be the last one to talk!"

She is about to say they aren't teenagers any more, that those details don't matter now, reminds herself that they do matter for her but stops herself. There were too many squabbles like that when they were children; now, when she needs him, is no time to start quibbling again.

He lets out a loud curse that makes her jump.

"*Shit de goddamn!* How stupid can you be? I sent the taxi away instead of keeping it here. Now I have to flag another one!"

It's an open taxi. After the streetcar where she was so cold, Maria decides she's totally unlucky. She is so cold, she's numb. The driver, with a coonskin hat and a pipe, doesn't seem to mind. He's taking his time, stopping too long at intersections for Maria's liking. She has pulled up her coat collar again but it's not enough. She feels her eyes running from the cold, what her mother used to call winter tears. As long as Ernest doesn't take them for tears of regret or shame. She gives him a surreptitious look. He has closed his eyes. You might think he's asleep. Maybe it's to avoid having to engage in conversation.

He reeks of alcohol. Despite the cold air rushing past, she can smell his drunken breath.

A little drink to give him courage before coming to meet her? One last shot "for the road" after quite a few shots since morning?

Immediately, she hates herself for her hasty judgment of him.

She called him in the middle of the evening, maybe he'd had a few glasses of beer with his food, what could be more normal? Why think the worst right away, jump to a hasty conclusion? She sighs. Because she knows that smell too well to disregard it, a smell that can't be mistaken, that she would recognize above any other. Gin. Not beer. Bols gin in its square green bottle that their father called four shoulders, another of the Desrosiers family's disasters. No. Not just the Desrosiers family ...

In a flash she is back in Maria at the Christmas Eve *réveillon* at the end of the last century, or a wedding or even a First Communion. The men all have dry throats, they sweat, they sing at the top of their lungs songs incomprehensible because they've been reworked by two centuries of illiterate performers; they ogle the girls – even their own father, the booming-voiced Méo Desrosiers, before his wife gave him an ultimatum, make a choice, booze or family, go back to the Lacordaire if he can't stop drinking on his own, or else – while the women hide their shame with meaningless chatter, keeping track of what's going on out of the corners of their eyes so things won't get out of hand. To avoid another tragedy they would then have to cover up, forgive, forget. Until next time. As usual. Bols gin-soaked breath. Maria's childhood was steeped in it and she found it again in New England, on most of the men she'd known. The poor man's panacea. Refuge of the hopeless. Even Monsieur Rambert, though he was such a reasonable man, was sometimes affected by it. Infected, like a disease.

She sees their father again raising those four shoulders, his dear, beloved bottle that he thinks is his salvation, holding it above his head, cheerful and panting like a seal. She can hear him shouting:

"Whey! It's like whey!"

He has tears from holding back, he's dying to bring to his lips what he calls his baby bottle because he can suck generous gulps for long seconds without stopping for breath, anxious to feel the poison run down his gullet, burn his insides, put his pain to sleep. Has her brother inherited their father's vice?

Yet Ernest is in the Mounted Police, he has a decent job, well paid, an enviable position that should keep him safe from all that – running away, the final shelter, the hole in the floor down through which he could disappear, the surrender of a person who has no choice but to drink to forget.

Their father again:

"Drown your sorrows, Maria. It's called drowning your sorrows. Drink is a bottomless lake that doesn't forgive. But it brings relief."

That morning he had just told his daughter that the glass he was holding was to be his last, or so he swore with his hand on his heart and all the rest. She knew he regretted it already, that he glimpsed with horror the months, the years that would follow – without his Bols gin to console him: the horror, the thirst, the suffering at being on the wagon without having chosen it himself.

"What am I going to drown my sorrows with, Maria? Water? Milk? Apple juice? A man needs something to get through life, Maria! He needs something that whomps him and numbs him and knocks him out!"

Despair. Greater than when he got down on his knees and begged forgiveness for beating them and, even more, for not remembering he had done so. How does he feel now after all those years? Her mother wrote that he was well, had never taken another drink, and that he was proud of himself. But can she believe her mother who always embellishes everything and is silent out of habit, it's second nature for her, what's really wrong? The refuge of alcohol for the father, protection by denial for the mother.

Maybe the presence of her granddaughters for five years now has helped her, who knows?

Has her father suffered through twelve years of not drinking?

And what pain can her brother, Ernest, be drowning with Bols gin?

"There's a surprise for you at our place."

She nearly jumps. She was beginning to think they wouldn't exchange a word till Ville-Émard.

"A surprise?"

"A big surprise."

"A good one or a bad one?"

"Depends how you take it."

Way to go, now she's scared.

After passing a warehouse whose name Maria could read in big letters – *Clos de Bois Jos Quesnel* – the taxi turns a corner, enters a dark street that cuts into Monk Boulevard, a blind alley that ends at a wooden fence, as if the world stopped there, in Ville-Émard. Maybe a warning. But about what?

Hot already. It's nothing compared with the dog days that afflicted Montreal in July – a whole week of suffocating heat that left Montrealers exhausted, sleep-deprived – but even now the air, heavy and damp, sticks to your skin and Rhéauna wonders what state she'll be in when she arrives at Windsor Station. At first she'd decided to walk; then she wondered if she ought to sacrifice a few cents to take the streetcar along St. Catherine Street. Spend a little money to save some time. And energy. She doesn't know where the station is exactly, just that it's at the other end of town, in the west, where hardly anybody speaks French, probably in the neighbourhood of Ogilvy's department store where her aunt Tititte works.

She has walked to Ogilvy's with her mother on other occasions, and found the walks to be fascinating because of everything they saw along the way, but mainly they had been exhausting: Maria was a fast walker, wasn't much interested in window-shopping though the shop windows they passed were magnificent; instead Maria kept telling her to hurry up even when they weren't in a hurry. Her mother hadn't walked, she'd *arrived*.

Rhéauna crosses Dorchester, which she has decided to leave because it's a street where nothing happens, an important thorough-fare for traffic but devoid of interest for a curious little girl: impatient pedestrians; cars that travel up to thirty miles an hour; buses that stink; carriages drawn by horses panic-stricken by so much activity; the danger of being run over at every intersection; and that was all.

She turns left at the corner of Montcalm and St. Catherine. The smell of horse manure and rotting garbage goes straight to her nose and she takes a handkerchief from her pocket. There are mornings like this when it is truly intolerable. Yet the city of Montreal isn't all that big. What must it be like in New York, or Paris, where they say in the papers and aunt Tititte confirms it, that in certain poor neighbourhoods in London animal dung is piled up at street corners, then sold to farmers who use it as fertilizer. Unless that's where legends originate intended to silence children who think that it stinks on the street. To make them understand that there are other places where it's worse. She often wonders why it is that horse manure smells so good in the country and so bad in town ... In Saskatchewan she would never have complained about the smell that scented the roads while here she finds it unbearable. Maybe the horses here don't eat the same thing or they don't digest the same way. The birds, though, don't seem to take offence the way they do in Maria, energetically pecking away at the road apples, searching for undigested seeds that they unearth by furious pecking and swallow, chirping happily.

Her shoes click on the wooden sidewalk, one of the last in town. She likes the sound; it reminds her of the big veranda surrounding her grandparents' house where she jumped rope all the time with Béa and Alice. She chants: *Mistress Mary, quite contrary, tell me the name of the boy I'll marry,* a nursery rhyme that accompanied one of her sisters' and her favourite games, a complicated thing where, while skipping rope, you had to find the initial of the one you would marry. You fixed it so that you'd cross your feet when you got to the initial letter in the first name of the last boy you'd chosen and, *voilà*, the deed was done, the marriage decided on, settled, dealt with, concluded. Even if it meant starting again the following week with another name. Rhéauna returns her handkerchief to her pocket. Her nose will get used to the odour, it always does. In a few minutes she won't smell a thing unless, of course, a horse does its thing right next to her. It's even worse when they pee. The monstrous thing that emerges from their bodies right on the street, in front of everybody, the powerful steaming gush that spatters everything, the smell of rotten eggs, the women who behave as if they haven't seen anything, the open mirth of the men who don't seem shocked by these things.

In the distance she spots the Dupuis Frères awning, at the

corner of St. Catherine and St. André, the unfashionable east-end counterpart to the department stores in the west of Montreal. She knows she's going to stop there, even suspects that she's made a detour for just that reason: she can't resist the wonders that await as soon as the doors of this Ali Baba cave full of miracles are open.

A loud noise draws Rhéauna's attention. A bottleneck has formed at the corner of Amherst and St. Catherine Streets, where a car trying to get around a horse and carriage has collided with a street lamp. Smoke pours out from under the car's hood, the motor stalls. The driver extricates himself from his seat, cursing like the damned, a crowd of onlookers begins to gather around him. He's asked how he is, if he was hurt, people offer their help; he's content to pile curse upon curse while taking off the cap and driving goggles that protect his head and his eyes against wind and dust. He tosses them onto the backseat of the car, then starts to furiously kick the street lamp. Rhéauna looks around in search of a space where she can edge her way between two automobiles or two streetcars. Traffic is paralyzed. No fewer than three streetcars wait at a standstill, each one stuck behind the other, car horns are blasting, horses neighing, women shouting for no reason, men laughing.

Yes, right there is a small space … But she hesitates because her mother has told her so many stories about children cut into pieces by the wheels of a streetcar, run over by an automobile because they'd tried to cross the street without going to an intersection. Nothing is moving apart from the increasingly agitated crowd, there's no real danger. She slips into the crowd, using her elbows to clear a path, manages to slip between two streetcars.

It's the first time she has slid between two contraptions the size of these. The air smells of electricity, a strange tingling sensation runs over her skin and on either side of her, she can make out the thrust of powerful engines. Beating hearts. Instead of hurrying to cross the street as quickly as possible as she knows she should do, she stops between the two vehicles, looks up, puts her hand on the metal that protects the engine from impact with the one behind, a huge vehicle painted dark green, with a threatening look. The metal is hot, it's vibrating, you would swear it was alive. She thinks of *Alice in Wonderland* which she has just read, though she understood practically nothing despite being fascinated by the fabulous characters and the strange adventures awaiting the heroine on every page, and also of the stories with valiant knights and dreadful dragons too, which kept her awake at night because a gigantic, fire-breathing lizard is quite terrifying. For several seconds she becomes one of those courageous knights and, using just the flat of her hand, she overcomes an electric dragon that could in fact make a mouthful of her as they say in those novels about gallant knights and terrible dragons. Her knight's tale is set in the eternal fog of England, a country permanently green, apparently because of the rain, and constantly drowned in the fog if you're to believe the novels set in the time of lords and ladies; but in Canada, in the bright August sun, a country with snow instead of fog, is far too young to have known the Middle Ages. It's not King Arthur with his sword Excalibur who charges the dragon of the fearsome Morgana Le Fey; no, it's the legendary Rhéauna Rathier who with her will alone has held back a streetcar on Montreal's St. Catherine Street! She feels at once powerful and weak; powerful because she can impose her will on a dangerous pile of scrap metal, weak because she wants to talk to it, confide in it, confess to it what she's is about to do, the absurd act that, yes, she suddenly realizes, with her hand on the muzzle of a dragon that can devour her in a second, will be of no help to her. Absolutely. Nothing. She suspected it, she thought about it even before leaving the house, but there before the baleful creature that growls but does not threaten, it's become obvious. Why had she taken off like that and why would she continue if she's so sure that it will serve no purpose? Absolutely. No purpose. Seven dollars and eleven cents to take three individuals across the entire continent! It's as absurd as *Alice in Wonderland*, isn't it? Or the battle between a knight and a dragon? She rests her forehead against the hot metal. Turn around? Or go on, all the way to the end, without a word to her mother about what she intends to do to protect them from the war, even if she knows in advance that her plan is doomed to fail. That's it! That's it, her reason for leaving, she'd forgotten! To protect them from the war. She herself, her brother, her mother. Keep forging ahead then. Without thinking, as in the novels about valiant knights and terrible dragons. So later she can reassure herself that at least she tried ... In adventure stories the valiant knight always succeeds in besting the dreadful dragon. But here, today, in 1914, the heroine is very weak and the war a very big monster to slay.

Some loud *klang-klang-klang*s remind her where she is, especially because the danger will be genuine if the streetcars start to move, and she jumps up onto the sidewalk. Thanks to a policeman who has come to sort out the traffic gridlock, waving his arms, cudgel in hand and whistle ready to blow, the streets are finally clear, traffic can start up again towards all four points of the compass. The driver of the damaged vehicle is alone in front of his car, scratching his head. He'll have to find himself a horse and carriage to pull him to the next garage, if there's one nearby, and feels humiliated because he knows they're going to laugh at him. For good reason.

Rhéauna looks at herself in a store window and thinks that she slightly resembles Alice in her dress that's nearly the same red – her mother had bought her the colour edition, which cost a lot more, that shows Alice in a pretty red dress and a white apron – but her dress is longer than the one in the novel because little girls in Montreal, obedient to the laws of the very strict Catholic church, must always look decent and wear dresses that come halfway down their calves, while if we're to believe the illustrations in *Alice in Wonderland*, little girls in England are allowed to look like real little girls. Reading the book, she envied Alice with her short, puffy dress, her big house, her garden, and her cat, Dinah. Rhéauna lives with her mother and her brother in an upstairs apartment without a garden and she's not allowed to have animals in the house, neither dogs nor cats, because her mother claims to be allergic to their hair. That may be just an excuse so she won't have to take care of them. Or not.

Rhéauna had a goldfish for a few months but she got tired of seeing it swim around and around in its bowl, open-mouthed and wild-eyed, and finally gave him his freedom by dropping him down the toilet. Who knows, maybe he's become a huge fish that lays down the law in the sewers of Montreal. Unless he was devoured by a rat the minute he swam out of the overflow pipe.

The fact remains that she doesn't have a cat, that Alice did, and she's still a little jealous. Rhéauna keeps walking quickly; she's nearly at Dupuis Frères, one of her favourite places in the world, and she can't wait to go up and down the broad aisles scented with so many exotic perfumes. It's the first leg in the journey that will lead her to Windsor Station.

Between Amherst and St. Timothy Streets – after a year she's still surprised at how many Montreal streets are named after saints – making herself as small as she can, she walks past the Chinese laundry of sinister reputation that makes all the children in the neighbourhood shiver. If you listened to the mothers in this poor part of town, then the laundry is a lair of bandits, kidnappers of children, and suppliers of young flesh for the white slave trade, which is apparently something horrible, that young girls disappear in a flash and are never seen again. They end up somewhere in China with a ruby in their belly buttons, doing things both dirty and reprehensible. Which doesn't stop the women in the neighbourhood from sending their children to pick up the laundry they've had washed. Even after they've said that the Chinese put their children to sleep with opium – a deadly drug that makes them crazy – then kill them, then chop them up to make soup that the family will eat with chopsticks, from bowls the size of soup kettles. All children who walk into the shop holding a small order form with Chinese characters handwritten on it, are terrorized, convinced that their final day has arrived and they tremble as they hold out their paper ticket. The Chinese don't speak French or English – or pretend not to – take their time going to find the order while the little customers stand by the door, ready to run away as soon as they see the tip of a knife or the shape of a ball of opium.

Rhéauna isn't sure she believes that legend, which would imply that mothers in the neighbourhood agree in full conscience to place their children's lives in danger. After all, they aren't in a tale by Hans Christian Andersen or the Brothers Grimm. But she never takes chances and tries every visit to stay as short a time as possible. Hold out the ticket, wait for the package, take out the money, grab the bundle of clean clothes, then run out to take refuge on the sidewalk, with the sound of streetcars spitting their sparks and automobiles sounding their horns, often for no reason.

But if it's just a legend, why make it up? Rhéauna wonders as she walks past the laundry, head down and suddenly determined to walk more quickly. She knows full well that certain stories exist to scare children, to stop them from misbehaving – but why that one? Why terrify a child before sending her out on an errand? So she won't drag her feet along the way? Mothers always understand, however, the moments of terror they pass on to their progeny, those moments of absolute horror imagining the handle of a long knife, blood spurting, the kettle of boiling water, the wooden chopsticks that dig around in bowls the size of soup kettles in search of pieces of children, well cooked? Or streets lost deep inside a distant Chinese province where you're required to do things too shameful to mention. If it's true, it's what wickedness really means. She would no doubt answer that it's just a joke, for laughs, that children shouldn't believe them … then tell them children should always believe their parents, who know the truth because they know more about life!

She takes refuge at Dupuis Frères under the awning that runs along the front of the store. Metal columns support a wrought-iron roof over which the upper storeys of the building cantilever, supported by corbels that extend the width of the canopy, right to the edge of the street. Which means that the sidewalk is protected from bad weather; in winter, there's hardly any accumulation of snow and, in summer, passersby are protected from the sun. Which is much appreciated by idlers and attracts customers, especially women, who otherwise would not have been tempted to enter the store.

Rhéauna recalls with delight the blessed day when her mother took her to Dupuis Frères for the first time. It was last year, she had barely arrived in Montreal and was complaining about the terrible big-city smells that choked her and made her sneeze non-stop.

Casually, Maria had told her that she was going to show her something amazing, a store like she had never seen, a vast establishment where you could find everything. Even order an elephant if you wanted. Rhéauna had stopped right in the middle of the sidewalk and looked up at her mother, who seemed to be enjoying her astonishment and holding back so she wouldn't burst out laughing.

"An elephant? You can buy an elephant at Dupuis Frères?"

"Sure. They say you just fill out an order form and then after a while you get your elephant ..."

"What can you do with an elephant in a house?"

"That doesn't mean people buy one, Nana, that children get one for Christmas! It just means you can if you want."

"Okay sure, but why would anyone buy an elephant?"

"That's an example, Rhéauna, just a way to say you can order anything at Dupuis Frères!"

"Oh sure, but why do they sell things nobody needs!"

"We don't know, Nana, maybe there are people who buy elephants, people with big houses, children who are spoiled brats ..."

Maria couldn't hold back any longer and let out a good laugh at her daughter's stupefied expression.

"Really, Nana, that was just an example I gave you; if I'd told you we were going to buy handkerchiefs, you wouldn't have paid any attention!"

Insulted, Rhéauna was now sulking and dragging her feet. She knew her mother hated that but wanted to make her pay for the trap she'd just set into which the girl had fallen like an idiot. Honestly! Buy an elephant! And she'd let herself be had!

Just before they went into the department store, Maria had said: "You'll see how wonderful it is."

And Rhéauna had stood there frozen like a fence post in front of what was unquestionably the most amazing, the most incredible, the most wonderful display of goods anyone could imagine. Outside was an inextricable jumble of automobiles and streetcars amid a deafening racket while here, inside an ordinary door you just had to push open, was an oasis of coolness and calm, a kind of general store like Mr. Connells's in the village of Maria but a thousand times bigger and even more bright and tidy.

An incalculable number of counters in every size were collapsing under tons of goods to be bought; chandeliers hung from the ceiling – well, not exactly chandeliers but close enough to be convincing; salesgirls all dressed the same way in long black skirts and immaculate white blouses ironed that morning were bustling around female clients often not as well dressed as they were – men were rare – offering them products covered in tissue paper that they took out with the greatest care from pretty cardboard boxes. Conversations were carried out *sotto voce*; heads topped with amazing hats were bent over glass display cabinets. Customers apparently not so rich, like Rhéauna and her mother, strolled around, trying to stay out of the spotlight. They dared not approach the counters and, with heads down and shoulders rounded, they avoided making eye contact with the saleswomen. But they devoured everything with their eyes, with furtive little glances since they couldn't get what they would have liked to take home.

And over it all reigned a mixture of soft, delicate perfume, scents vastly different from those Rhéauna had put up with since her arrival in Montreal, a fusion of flowers and plants so subtle it brought tears to her eyes. It smelled at once of windswept fields and exotic flowers worn by women who could afford them. She found fragrant Saskatchewan sweetgrass as well as a flower whose name she's forgotten that she'd discovered on the neck of the great Ti-Lou in Ottawa. Had she been able to afford it, she'd have known how to obtain the scent and wear it all the time.

Maria leaned over and laid one hand on her daughter's shoulder.

"I knew you'd be impressed, Nana."

Impressed? She'd have loved to settle there, under a counter or behind a column, never leave the store so as to feel far away from the foul smells of the big city and imagine being back at the Château Laurier in Ottawa, in the arms of the most beautiful woman she had ever seen in her life and who had been so kind to her.

Since that day, since that guided tour with her mother through Dupuis Frères with its numerous departments that were crammed with splendours whose existence she hadn't even suspected, every time she has the opportunity Rhéauna haunts the aisles in this concentration of all that is most beautiful in the world. She doesn't meet an elephant of course, but she sees lots of things she'd never have thought you could buy in an ordinary general store, like furniture for the whole house or underwear for women displayed where everyone can see it, perfumes that salesgirls had made her try, giggling too, perfumes in small bottles with incredible shapes that filled dozens and dozens of racks. Her pleasure is intact, she feels the same excitement over the discoveries she makes on every one of her visits, especially when a saleslady holds out a pretty coloured bottle with a rubber atomizer bulb that releases an aroma that will follow her all day long and that triggers her imagination. She runs from floor to floor, her curiosity first stirred then fulfilled every time, and she knows that she will never exhaust the wonders hiding in every nook and cranny of the magnificent hodgepodge. She doesn't want to buy anything, she wants to *look* at everything, wondering what you would do with all that stuff, filling her eyes and nose and making her head swim with memories that later on she will try to bring back to life.

Her mother had tousled her hair.

"Smells good, doesn't it? Here's where your aunts and I found our Tulipe Noir … Look, that's the saleslady waiting on a customer. She's really nice. Jeannine Cusson. Even though it doesn't cost much, she never looks down on me when I come to buy a bottle."

Rhéauna takes up a position at the store's main entrance, pressing her nose against it before opening the door. Right away, she sees Jeannine Cusson smiling behind her counter, even though there's no one in front of her begging for samples or seeking advice. She also notices Monsieur Simoneau, the house detective, who seems to have taken a dislike to her some time ago; now he's decided to follow her around whenever he notices her. This morning he's prowling the perfume department, on the lookout for the slightest suspicious move, devoured by the need to arrest someone. It's especially ridiculous because the store is nearly empty this early in the morning. Rhéauna can't help sketching a little smile. Look, the Big Bad Wolf. She is no longer Alice, now she is Little Red Riding Hood.

She pushes open the door and plunges into this fantastic universe of light and aroma, where exotic scents seem to emerge from books she has read and that have made her dream: is that the smell of the Arabia in the *Thousand and One Nights* she's now reading, not suspecting that it's a watered-down edition for children, or is it the scent of the Ancient Egypt of the Pharaohs, where it is said cosmetics were invented; is it the perfume Cleopatra was about to spray on herself when the asp bit her; or the one Delilah sported – she has just learned that use of the word *sport* and tries to include it in conversation as often as she can even if it means making a mistake – when she cut Samson's hair? Or that scent of new-mown grass, is it the one that drifted around the den of the White Rabbit, who was in such a hurry when Alice encountered him and then slid down the hole in her pretty red dress, but only after she'd told her cat, Dinah, not to follow her because it might be dangerous? Or is it the one that Little Red Riding Hood inhaled when she entered the threatening forest, her little basket under her arm? Ah, that's the name she's been trying to find, the scent worn by Ti-Lou, her older cousin, warm and pungent, that brings a lump to her throat. The lovely Mademoiselle Cusson – she's obliged to call her Mademoiselle Cusson in front of customers, but to her she will always be the lovely Jeannine – told her it was made with a base of gardenia, another beautiful word to remember and to savour, a pure white flower so fragile it lasts only a few days and is worth a fortune. Especially because Jeannine had been ordered to hand out samples sparingly, just to wealthy customers who were likely to buy some. Rhéauna understood and didn't press her. Anyway, she doesn't feel ready yet – or mature enough – to *sport* gardenia. Gardenia is for the grand life: Ottawa, the Château Laurier, horse-drawn carriages, mechanical staircases, big hats, ankle boots made of soft leather. And the blaring of men who knock on the door in the middle of the night for some mysterious reason.

Jeannine is glad to see her but nods in the direction of Monsieur Simoneau, who at the moment has his back turned to them.

"I have to tell you, he's in a bad mood today. Unbearable. He seems to be mad at the whole world!"

She bends down behind her counter, takes out a rather ugly flask shaped like a scallop shell.

"Do you want to try this? It just came in. Sea Breeze. It's a nice name but I'm not sure I like it … Anyway, it had me sneezing for five minutes."

She holds the bottle in one hand, the bulb between thumb and index finger in the other, head leaning backwards, ready to plunge Nana into a new olfactory adventure, but the little girl holds her back.

"If you don't like it I'd rather not try it … I don't want to smell like fish or the devil for the rest of the day."

When they burst out laughing, Monsieur Simoneau turns around at once, convinced they're talking about him behind his back.

"What's so funny?"

They look at each other, blush, burst out laughing again, then cover their faces with both hands. Two little girls caught red-handed. Jeannine is first to catch her breath.

"We were just laughing at the name of a new perfume, Monsieur Simoneau."

"I see. And what's the name of that perfume?"

"Sea Breeze."

"Sea Breeze. What's so funny about that?"

They hang their heads, suddenly ashamed. Why ashamed, Rhéauna wonders. Why let themselves be impressed by this fat man bursting out of his clothes, who is trying to start a fight because he has nothing else to do and who tries to get involved with perfumes but knows nothing about them?

Strictly from bravado, to stand up to him, put him in his place, or all three at the same time, she straightens up and says to Jeannine, with an accent she would like to sound French but that sounds more like the one her aunt Tititte uses when she tries to speak well at Ogilvy's before a lady from Outremont:

"You shall let me have a case of it, Mademoiselle Cusson, I intend to bathe in it this very afternoon, while sipping hot chocolate."

He's on her before she even thinks to react.

"Listen, you, you aren't going to laugh at me again!"

She raises her hand as if to surrender.

"Excuse me. I was rude. But it's true we weren't talking about you, Monsieur Simoneau ..."

She gives him her prettiest smile, the one she thinks is irresistible because it made her grandparents melt back home in Maria, but which her mother has shown herself to be impervious to this past year. So it's not infallible, though it does work on strangers who think it's sincere.

Disconcerted, the security officer straightens up too, clears his throat, steps back a few paces.

"At least you've got some manners, you know enough to excuse yourself."

Even broader, the smile. And batting her eyes always has an effect.

"I'm going to look at the toys on the fourth floor ... I saw a doll I sort of liked the other day. Bye, Mademoiselle Cusson ... Bye, Monsieur Simoneau. Excuse me again."

She turns her back and walks away from the perfume department, leaving both of them open-mouthed, one behind her counter, the other in the middle of the aisle.

Jeannine hides her giggles behind her hand. As for Monsieur Simoneau, suspecting that he's once again let himself be manipulated, he raises his arm as if he's intending to whack the little brat.

There are more customers in the store now. Rhéauna decides to follow two young women in hats and gloves who are on their way to the wooden staircase that leads to the upper floors. They chatter, laughing, and don't stop at any of the displays; they must know exactly where they are headed. Rhéauna decides to follow them, just to see what the two pretty women are coming to buy so early in the morning. As they tackle the stairs, they lift their skirts with one hand and, with the other, hold on to the handrail, still gabbing. The taller lady, the one on the right, is wearing boots such as Rhéauna has never seen. Lower than the ones imposed by decency, with heels too high to be comfortable, they seem cut from a leather so soft and supple that they fit the ankle and hug the feet like gloves. Foot gloves. Rhéauna smiles. *Foot gloves.* It's a nice expression, she should keep it in mind to use when she needs it.

On the third floor, the two customers stop in the underwear department. Rhéauna stays frozen in the aisle, unsure what to do. An eleven-year-old child has no reason to linger among counters covered with bloomers, cotton undershirts in every size, and pale-pink corsets. She dares not look too closely at what the headless wooden mannequins around her have on. She walks past the two customers who now are bending over a pile of undergarments she can't see but that seem to be made of foamy white lace. They may be women like Ti-Lou, women who practise a profession very different from her mother's and very obviously take from it much more money than she does. Do they also live in a grand hotel, a *sweet* that smells of gardenias, with a bed too big for one person, and a bathroom as huge as the kitchen in the apartment on Montcalm Street.

Something very funny has likely just been said because the two women burst out laughing. A saleswoman, rather elderly, stiff, her bust uplifted, a slightly contemptuous look on her face, approaches them, asks them in a tone at the very edge of politeness what they are looking for. What the taller one replies, which Rhéauna, too far away, can't quite hear, seems to scandalize the saleswoman intensely. She brings her hand to her vast bosom, closing her eyes. The two women walk past Rhéauna without even glancing at her. They could have told her she's pretty in her red dress, couldn't they? It's her prettiest dress, her Sunday best, and she knows that she's ravishing!

She decides she's had enough of those two brainless idiots who don't see anything but their own little selves – they're not nearly as interesting as she'd thought at first – and makes her way towards the saleswoman who has her hand on her heart and now is leaning against the counter. What could they have said to her to put her in such a state?

"Are you okay, Madame?"

The saleswoman straightens up, runs her hands through her hair, which is done up in a complicated twist that must take hours to construct.

"Yes sure, I'm okay. It's just those two lunatics that ..."

Trembling, she rearranges the pile of mysterious white lace undergarments.

"Never mind, there are some things you just don't say in front of children."

One more reason to know them! But Rhéauna guesses it would be pointless to insist, that the lady is too upset, so instead heads for the staircase that will take her to the toy department.

It's a gorgeous Japanese doll that Rhéauna comes to look at now and then, to admire her beautiful sea-green dress with its enormous yellow silk sash tied in the back, her head and hands in painted porcelain, her features so fine, so delicate, drawn with a few precise strokes of the pen. No one seems to want her because she is still there on her display stand, dignified and upright, protected by a bright-red parasol that clashes prettily with the colours of her costume. Rhéauna has been content to admire her from afar for weeks now, ever since she went under glass to keep overly curious little girls from touching her. What a pleasure it would be to take care of her, to carry her all over, to invent a story about her as an unhappy woman who is being held prisoner far from home, strange adventures they would play together in an invented language because Rhéauna doesn't know a thing about Japan except that it's very far away, at the other end of the earth, in Asia, next to China, that everyone who lives there has slanted eyes and speaks an incomprehensible language. They understand one another of course, but no one else can understand *them*. When they speak together it may sound something like the funny language used by the Chinese at the laundry. The girl would invent a language, then, that only she and the doll could decipher, one that would cut them off from the rest of the world. They would confide their woes in their secret language and maybe they would be not so sad. Rhéauna borrowed old rags from her mother and her flowered umbrella to make herself a costume something like her doll's – it's called a kimono so the word must come from Japan – she would move into her room with Théo on her lap and Japan, a mysterious land in Asia, next to China, would appear before their eyes.

The saleswoman approaches, hands on hips.

"You again. You like that doll a lot, don't you?"

Awakened from her daydreams, Rhéauna merely shrugs and walks away, sighing.

She strolls among the counters, picks up a few dolls, particularly a smiling baby that she rocks, calling it Théo, then suddenly remembers that she's not there to play dolls, that her visit to Dupuis Frères is just an impromptu detour in her long expedition to Windsor Station, that she'd gone into the store to fill her nostrils with pleasant aromas before braving the other more aggressive and inconvenient smells of St. Catherine Street, and nothing else. She has no time to waste, however; she has to be home before noon.

She puts back the baby doll next to the dozen of its rubber twins, all decked out with the same frozen smile, and starts running for the stairs. And it is there, on the landing of the toy department, that Little Red Riding Hood comes face-to-face with the Big Bad Wolf.

"Where're you going in such a big hurry?"

"I have an errand to run, Monsieur Simoneau, and I'd forgotten ..."

"Your mother sends you out to do errands and you come and waste your time at Dupuis Frères playing with dolls?"

"My errand was here, but on a different floor."

She tries to go around him to rush onto the stairs, leave the place, run. But he's blocking the way.

"Wait! Wait! I'm not done!"

"But I'm in a hurry, I have to do my errand and my mother's waiting for me at home."

"She can wait a few more minutes."

He leans over her. He is almost obliged to bend double because he's so much taller. She can smell his breath, the breath of someone who doesn't brush his teeth very often, and she moves back a few steps. He tips his head to the side, a little like a dog that doesn't fully understand what he's just been told or who thinks it's mealtime.

"Would you be a little thief by chance?"

She's startled. She didn't expect to be accused like this, she definitely hasn't done anything to provoke such an insinuation, she's frozen there, open-mouthed, stunned. Rhéauna, a thief? Where could that idea have come from? And where could she have hidden anything; all she has on her is her little shoulder bag in which she certainly couldn't have hidden anything as big as a doll.

"Are you a little thief?"

His expression is weird. It's as if his eyes have charged ahead of him, in that they now protrude a little more than before.

"What're you hiding? And where are you hiding it?"

She has to reply, prove to him she hasn't stolen anything so he'll let her by. Panicking, she opens her purse.

"You can see I'm not hiding anything. I haven't got room to hide anything in here."

"What's all that money for? There's tons of money in that bag!"

"I told you I'm doing errands for my mother."

"Pretty big errands, eh! How much have you got there? Ten bucks? Twenty?"

He's not going to confiscate the money from her piggy bank that it took her a whole year to collect!

"I haven't got ten dollars, I've just got seven dollars and eleven cents."

She immediately regrets having spoken. Why did she tell him the exact amount? Idiot! She let out *the* thing she should have kept silent, *the* detail that will be her undoing.

Monsieur Simoneau frowns, licks his lips.

"Seven bucks and eleven cents! That's pretty precise!"

Quick! Come up with a reply! Quick!

"She sent me to buy stuff that costs exactly seven dollars and eleven cents."

He seems to be enjoying himself, the repulsive creep.

"Is that so? What is it that costs exactly seven bucks and eleven cents? In what department? On what floor?"

She stands there in front of him, silent and paralyzed. What could cost that exact amount? She doesn't have the foggiest idea.

Before she even tries to launch into something like an explanation, he grabs her by the nape of her neck.

"I don't know what you're hiding but I'm sure going to find out ... Come into my office, we'll see."

She struggles, whomps him with her purse, but he's too strong for her and tightens the pressure of his fingers around her neck. Turning around she spots the saleslady from the toy department who is looking at them, arms crossed over her meagre bosom. Why does she not come and help her? She can't think the girl is a thief too! And let Monsieur Simoneau take her into his office! But the saleslady doesn't say a word, merely knits her brow before she turns her head and walks away. Rhéauna realizes then that all are suspect, that it's not the first time this kind of incident has occurred, that Monsieur Simoneau definitely doesn't think she's a thief and that he has to come up with some other excuse. She thinks about everything her mother has been telling her about men in the past year, the danger of talking to strangers, the threat that lies in wait for little girls who are too bright, the significance of a story like *Little Red Riding Hood* in a big city like Montreal ... She starts to tremble. She wants to scream but can't. She starts to cry because her neck hurts. They head for the stairs that lead to the ground floor and take them four at a time. Monsieur Simoneau guides her, drags her rather, to the back of the store, under the mezzanine where the ceiling is low and the air stifling, behind the school supplies, to the precise spot where she'd told her mother she was going ... That's it! That's what she should have told him! Seven dollars and eleven cents' worth of supplies for school that starts next week!

What's going to happen to her? What's going to happen?

Her heart is pounding, she has to pee. No one comes to help her. Customers and saleswomen watch them pass but don't say a word. Another little thief who deserves what lies ahead for her. Rhéauna wants to yell at them:

"It's not the police he wants to call! It's not the police! Help me!" but her throat is tight and she stays mute. With terror.

The storage room Monsieur Simoneau uses as an office reeks of sweat, cigarettes, and unwashed clothes. It's not an office, it's hardly bigger than a cubbyhole and probably it's only used when the security guard catches "thieves." Innocent like her or not.

He closes the door before he sets Rhéauna free. The little girl at once takes refuge behind the small table that takes up most of the space.

"Why did you close the door? Don't close it!"

The stale air in this tiny interrogation room is oppressive, Rhéauna has trouble breathing. She feels as if she's being poisoned, she's going to suffocate, she's going to vomit ... Her heart is pounding, sweat is running down her back. She's going to soil her pretty red dress! Because a crazy man thinks she's a thief!

Monsieur Simoneau creeps up to her. His tone of voice is softer now but, in a way, more menacing too: now the two are alone, no one will witness their conversation so he can risk using the patronizing and superior tone of someone who knows he can't lose. He seems to be savouring this incident that he himself has provoked. Rhéauna is convinced that he knows she hasn't stolen anything, that he's doing this for fun, out of sheer nastiness. Or for some other still mysterious reason.

"Are you going to tell me what you stole, you little thief in a red dress. Are you? And are you going to show me where you hid it, where you hid what you stole? Are you? Or do I have to go and get it myself?"

He holds out his hand, he's going to feel her all over, on her clothes, maybe even underneath. She can already imagine his dirty paws on her back, her thighs, her bum, his poisoned breath on her neck, her mouth ... Suddenly she feels a knot of anger form in her belly. It comes from deep inside, it's cold, hard, violent, it keeps her from breathing, but it also gives her the courage to react, which she wouldn't have had if she'd given herself over to fear as he'd most likely expected. That's how he must operate: first he scares his victims, threatens them, and then he can do whatever he wants with them because they don't dare resist him, he represents the law, justice, he is the stronger of the two …

So then she starts to scream. It's the strident cry of a desperate child who doesn't know any other way to express her terror, a piercing sound that cuts through the door of Monsieur Simoneau's office, then scatters all over the ground floor of the department store. Sound the alarm. Using every means possible. Warn everyone. About the danger. About the danger of this lunatic who has been entrusted with responsibilities he doesn't deserve.

Monsieur Simoneau is startled, surprised at the reaction of Rhéauna, who takes advantage of a few seconds of hesitation to turn her cries into accusations.

"Why did you shut the door? Eh? Why did you shut the door? You don't have to shut the door to ask me questions!"

Suddenly she pushes the big man even though he smells so bad, like the drunks who make her wrinkle her nose when she sometimes meets them on the street. She walks around him, grabs the knob, opens the door. She could go out, run away, but reassured by the presence of several customers who came running when they heard her howling, she turns towards them with her hand on her heart.

"Aren't you ashamed? You stinking pig! Rotten stinking pig! What would you have done if I hadn't screamed, eh? With the door shut! What were you going to do to me?"

Actually she doesn't know what he wanted to do to her, her mother hasn't yet had the mother-daughter conversation that the nuns at her school have talked about in veiled terms for months, about relations between men and women. What she does know, however, is that those things must not happen in a storage room at the back of a department store between a fake policeman who stinks and a terrified little-girl customer. But what? What? What is it? Who does what? How do they do it?

She lets herself get carried away by her own words.

"That money was to buy my school supplies, you know! I broke my piggy bank to buy school supplies and you have no right to ask me questions like a thief. In a room that stinks and with the door shut!"

Mouth open, he sits on his little table. He doesn't even think of wiping the sweat that has started to run down his forehead, on his cheeks, even on his neck. Besides, his hanky must be grimy and he would make himself even dirtier.

Rhéauna takes advantage of this momentary calm to make a run for it. She clears a passage through the women cramming the aisles of the store and heads for the exit, freedom. Panicking, she crosses the entire ground floor with fear in her belly, ears buzzing, and she calls out to Mademoiselle Cusson as she runs past the perfume counter:

"Are there police to arrest police? If there are, call them up right away! Monsieur Simoneau is crazy!"

Rhéauna pushes open the double door and ends up under the marquee, sheltered from the August sun beating down. The air is thick, the humidity that has settled over Montreal like a bell jar makes everything in her field of vision vibrate: the passing streetcar makes her think of something soft that she could knead between her hands, the horses look fake because the light is too harsh, the crowd might just as well be an assembly of ghosts without substance.

She continues racing till she reaches the corner of St. Hubert Street, where she collapses onto a wooden bench. She looks in the direction from whence she came. No. No one is following her. The phony policeman may be talking to a real Montreal policeman right now. Or if the phony policeman hasn't dared to protest, maybe Mademoiselle Cusson is talking to a real Montreal policeman.

Doubt takes hold of her as quickly as anger did just a moment before. And what if he'd been sincere? If he had really thought she'd stolen something? If after all he'd only been doing his job? He isn't guilty just because he stinks! Not at all. But his eyes weren't normal, they were crazy eyes. Heaven above! But what if she were wrong?

And what will she do when she goes back to Dupuis Frères? Is she sentenced never to set foot there again? Even with her mother?

Rhéauna feels a great fatigue. She should turn around, go home, take refuge in the peace and quiet of the apartment on Montcalm Street, with her little brother's giggling and her mother's reprimands. A little girl isn't supposed to run down the street like that, go out in search of adventures over which she has no control. She was lucky just now but it might not happen again ... And once more she shudders at the thought of the war marching ever nearer. She thinks about her grandparents' house, so far away and so safe from any danger, about her sisters whose laughter and shouts of excitement she's dying to hear when they arrive – herself, her brother, their mother – and she straightens up on her bench. An illusion. It's true that it's just an illusion. But a wonderful illusion. One that she must follow to the very end.

Three ladies were standing in front of Maria in the long corridor that cut the apartment in two. Neat and tidy. Somewhat stiff. The oldest, most likely Alice, Ernest's wife, had the vague expression of an alcoholic halfway between being controllably tipsy and hopelessly drunk. She knew where she was but for how long? She was standing upright, shoulders back, bust high, neck stretched. It was obvious though that her posture required a nearly superhuman effort and that at any moment it could all collapse. The cloak of decorum, the makeup required by propriety, would then give way to rambling and erratic gestures. Maria grasped all this in just a few seconds because this tiny woman reminded her of her husband and the rest of the Rathier family, whose get-togethers often took place amid that warning state of sobs of self-pity or gratuitous violence. So *that* was what her brother had married? Poor man. He was no better off than she herself had been. She didn't recognize the others right away. Two small women in their thirties who could just as well have been forty or fifty, so much did their attire, though well cared for, come from another age: dress a little too long, shoulders a little too wide, lace collar on the one on the left, the pudgy one; bouffant sleeves on the other, the more elegant, a bitter fold at the corner of the lips, and worried brows in both cases. Women who had lived through difficult times, whose hearts had hardened prematurely. Like her, like the woman she saw in the mirror when she was getting ready for the day. Pretty, though, impressive in their affected dignity that did not, however, fool anyone. And strangely familiar. Those beautiful faces, the domed foreheads, the planes of the cheeks characteristic of ...

Maria brought her hands to her heart.

Eyes close together set high on the face, bronzed complexion, the taller one with dimples ...

Ernest cleared his throat before he spoke.

"You're lucky you came on our poker night."

Tititte! Teena!

She closed her eyes.

It's summer. Very hot. It hasn't rained for weeks and brush fires have started to wreak havoc around the small village of Maria. All five of them are sitting on the veranda of the big white house to take a little fresh air before going to bed. Joséphine has made lemonade with the only lemon she could find at Monsieur Connells's, Méo has been smoking his damn pipe which smells too strongly of vanilla. As for the three Desrosiers sisters, Tititte, Teena, and Maria, they are bickering about a young man from Saskatoon; for a while now he's been visiting their village rather often and it's said that he is looking for a wife. He's a good catch, apparently, son of a wealthy farmer, and the marriageable girls are all excited. Except Maria Desrosiers, of course.

"You don't find a wife by visiting villages, for Pete's sake! You make it sound as if he wants to buy a winter coat! Is he going to check our teeth, dig around in our hair to see if we have lice? There's a difference, you know, between wanting to find a wife and buying one in the back of beyond because it will be cheaper."

Tititte, the dreamiest but also the oldest, thinks it's romantic that a stranger is criss-crossing country roads just like that, in search of one to love. Here, most of the time marriages are arranged between both sets of parents in the same parish, and the bride and groom know each other far too well when they arrive at the church because they've grown up together.

"I'd like it if a man showed up out of the blue like that and …"

"… and carried you away on his white steed?"

"Why not? In fact I'd be happy with any colour of horse, even an old nag."

Maria bursts out laughing.

"And handsome and not dangerous!"

Tititte straightens.

"Don't laugh! I'm serious!"

"Which is exactly why I'm laughing."

She lays her hand on her sister's shoulder.

"Just about anything to get out of here, right, Tititte?"

"That's not what I said ..."

"... but it's what you meant."

"It was not."

"You claim you don't believe me when I shriek that I want to get out of this place at any cost, but you wish you had the courage to do it too, don't you?"

Teena breaks in before the conversation can become toxic. She knows her sisters and she senses the coming of the break, the moment when this conversation would transform into an endless squabble that their mother would have a terrible time getting under control because Maria and Tititte could never agree. About anything.

"Cut it out, you two, you'll make me drop a stitch!"

Teena holds up a shapeless piece of knitting she's been working on for weeks that she'll probably give up on while her sisters look on, disdainful. It's a pattern her mother had ordered from a catalogue, the one from Eaton's, the nicest one, telling her it was easy to follow and then she'd have a warm wool sweater for winter. The wool was midnight blue, the needles a little too big. Teena has no talent for knitting and what she is fiddling with this evening on the veranda, to please Joséphine, looks more like a winter coat for a dog than a woollen sweater she could display with pride at High Mass on Sunday.

"If you don't cut it out I'll make *you* wear it." And she holds out the knitting in their direction.

Maria grabs it, turns it over on all sides.

"Maybe if you put it on your head people will think it's a winter hat." Which she does. She holds it, stretches it, and pulls it over her head. The two sleeves – of different lengths – fall on either side of her face; someone might think it's the dog from the neighbouring farm whose ears are too long and who always moans when he walks because his feet hurt.

"Anyway, that thing on my head won't make Prince Charming notice me!"

Maria treats them to some silly remarks, imitates Madame Chartier's dog, Beauty, a bad name for him when he stumbles over his long, drooping ears.

Everyone has a good laugh, the storm blows over, disaster is once again avoided thanks to Maria's shenanigans.

Before she opens her eyes, Maria wonders if that's what they expect of her: that she will find some comical reply, a gag to lighten the atmosphere, that she will change the subject of the painful conversation that's liable to start up, as she felt obliged to do for so long when she was a child? Erase twelve years of separation with a provocative remark? Act as if no time had passed, that she hadn't married, that she hadn't had three children, that she wasn't expecting another one, ignore the fact that the years had not been kind to her sisters and claim that all was well? Or play child prodigy with her head down and shoulders hunched? In the hope that she'll be forgiven? No, that's out of the question. She feels trapped, even though she knows that her sisters would never have time to cross the city to come and wait for her in the depths of Ville-Émard unless Ernest had advised them. She has come to ask a single person for help and here she is in front of nearly the entire family gathered around a poker table, plus that alcoholic woman who's going to fall on her face any minute if no one holds her up. So many hours being shaken up on the train to end up here, surrounded by the smell of cabbage soup combined with cigar smoke!

She feels sick to her stomach, she's going to throw up, she needs to ask for the bathroom.

And after not seeing her brother or her sisters for twelve years, these are the first words she utters. Without opening her eyes:

"Can you tell me where the bathroom is? I feel a little woozy."

Ernest takes her by the arm, Tititte and Teena bustle about around her – she can guess from the rustling of dresses and the sweetish perfume, which is more intense in the corridor, accentuating her nausea.

"Come, it's this way … Do what you have to, then come back … I've got a good medicine if you have trouble swallowing … It was Alice told me about it … Doesn't taste very good but it works … There's a big bottle in the medicine chest."

She'd like to yell at him that the trouble isn't with her digestion, that she's expecting a baby she doesn't want, that she's decided to keep it and start a new life. Here. In Montreal. With his help. Not the women's. That she actually even wished that Tititte and Teena didn't know she'd come back. For the time being at least. Even though you couldn't call it a return because she'd never set foot in Montreal. After so many years, all the Desrosiers had ended up in Montreal, the final refuge, the place that in the past their family had left in search of a better life. A better life! Hell, yes! Slavery! Disgrace! Contempt …

She hopes they can't hear her belching, spitting, fingers of one hand on her throat and the other holding a cool cloth to her forehead.

Too bad. She has the right to be sick.

She gets up, runs the washcloth over her face. Then looks in the mirror. She hasn't aged as much as her sisters, has she? But she sees her face every day, they don't. What did they think when they saw her? "Here's the floozy back in town! God almighty, look how she's aged! What kind of life has she been living?" "For sure she needs money." Yes. That's true. She needs money. And work. And an apartment. A room, in any case … She has rested her elbows on the edge of the sink that smells of mints because, without a doubt, Alice comes here to mask the alcohol on her breath.

And she cries. At the absurdity of her plan. At her own foolishness. At the dead-end situation she's thrown herself into.

Ernest has twice knocked on the door.

"Are you okay, Maria?"

What can she say? Everything's perfect? Life is beautiful? There's no sense waiting because she has piles of new stories to tell them, each one funnier than the others. Life of the party, again? The clown?

She merely emits a grunt that could pass for assent. Then she sits on the rim of the toilet. She'd have liked to lie on her back in the tub, arms crossed on her bosom, like a dead woman in her tomb. And to let warm water run onto her in an endless stream. Warm water that would stop time and finally put her to sleep. Forever.

She'll do it, she has almost lifted a foot to step into the tub when a woman's voice speaking English comes to her through the door.

"Maria? This is Alice, your sister-in-law. Do you need anything? Open the door, please."

Then she starts to laugh. It's amazing, it comes from deep inside, it's exhausting, but she feels relieved of the intolerable burden that's been weighing on her heart since she left Providence. Basically it's all funny, isn't it? Maria's own silliness, her naivety, her bird's brain unable to think about the consequences of her behaviour.

She unlocks the medicine chest, opens the half-empty bottle of indigestion medicine, and takes a long swig. An appalling taste fills her mouth and immediately she starts to vomit again. Still laughing.

When she pulls open the bathroom door, her two sisters are waiting for her in the corridor. Not Ernest. Or his wife. Her sisters are still erect in their outmoded wardrobes. This time, though, Maria reads in their eyes a nuance she hasn't seen before. Compassion? Affection? They are frowning, yes, but she doesn't sense that they are judging her.

Teena crosses the corridor, puts her hand on Maria's shoulder.

"You sure get over things fast, Maria. A real jack-in-the-box. What's going on?"

Tititte does the same but it is Maria's forearm that she strokes.

"We don't hear a word from you for twelve years then suddenly you're back from the ends of the earth with no warning to us, one night in October. And the first thing you do when you get here is throw up in the toilet! We're worried, Maria, really worried. And so's Ernest."

Worried? Their clan's main activity! She thought that part of her life – her existence with the Desrosiers, her separation from them, her flight, the new life she had first thought was wonderful, far from Saskatchewan, but had turned out to be disappointing – had been settled once and for all. She had never, ever wanted to hear from them so why are they worried about her? But hadn't Ernest used his contacts in the Mounted Police to track her down a few months earlier? Tititte and Teena must know, it was a proof of interest if not affection, wasn't it? So it was her in the end, she was the heartless one who didn't want to hear anything about them during all that time, not them.

She leaned back against the bathroom door she'd just shut behind her so that the odours she had left there couldn't escape. She folded her arms and made eye contact with each one in turn as she used to do as a child when she was about to tell a whopper. Tititte and Teena, not taken in, moved back a step.

Maria, the rebel, the dreamer, had come back, anything could happen. Especially something unpleasant.

She spoke very softly but without looking down.

"I'm expecting my fourth baby. With a man I'm not married to. And I don't know what to do. Ernest offered to help out if I had any problems … So now I've got one. One hell of a problem."

To say that the silence was long would be diluting the truth. In fact it stretched out between them for several long minutes. It was as if Maria's words were still ringing in the house, that they were bouncing off the walls; you would hear them for years, the numerous occupants of the apartment who would follow Ernest and Alice would be able to hear Maria recite her confession, admit the unspeakable in this society in which giving birth outside marriage was an unforgivable crime.

"Say something, somebody!"

She hadn't raised her voice, only asked them to react to a revelation that she'd guessed would be terrible for them.

Tititte ran her hands through her hair, smoothing it upwards as if to tuck away a lock that hadn't moved.

"What can we say, poor dear? You're a widow and you're pregnant, it's not simple."

"I didn't say it was simple and in fact I know it isn't. I just said that I needed help."

Ernest's voice came to them from the living room.

"I know you haven't seen one another for a long time, but that's enough chit-chat!"

They respond automatically to the sound of his voice, as they did when they were little and he got them to obey him by shouting. They head for the living room without touching one another.

The minuscule room is filled with oversize furniture: a monstrous sofa, dark red with a design of acanthus leaves, is flanked by twin bottle-green wing chairs that take up most of the available space. A long, low table sits in front of the sofa, and its occupants, Alice and Ernest, have to bend their knees while keeping their legs so close to the jigsawed base that they hit their shins. The opaque curtains masking the window are also green and red. A few pictures depicting panoramas of the Canadian west – Lake Louise, the Rockies, a street in Banff – hang too high on the walls. The room is stifling and it smells of cheap cigars. A festive window – all that green, all that red! – left to its fate, the colours faded. Like old and worn out Christmas decorations. The window is closed so the air in the room is too dry and Maria is afraid her nausea will come back.

As her two sisters have taken the armchairs, Maria is left standing in the middle of the room: an accused person in front of her judges. There would be room between her brother and her sister-in-law on the massive sofa but they would be squeezed and she would be looking at everyone in profile as well. And what she's about to confide to them has to be said directly to their faces.

Though it has gone out, Ernest sighs as he tamps his cigar in the ashtray placed near him on a small table with a tall *torchère* in metal and frosted glass looking down on it.

"You aren't going to stay on your feet like that … Teena, go get a chair from the kitchen."

He isn't speaking to his wife, who in any case would be hard-pressed to bring a chair from the kitchen to the living room in the state she is in. She seems to be asleep with her eyes open. Not one muscle moves, her eyes are staring, she is plainly lost in an alcoholic mist and no doubt is happy to escape from the depressing reality of this stifling living room disguised all year long as a Christmas tree.

"No, no, Teena, never mind I'll get it ..."

Walking through the apartment, Maria can't help taking a good look around. Everything is heavy, dark, depressing. The bedroom is as overcrowded as the living room – the double bed seems too narrow for two people so overwhelming is everything around it – and the kitchen, clean and bright as a new penny, has no personality: it's functional, unimaginative, and ugly.

She lifts a wooden chair, it's too heavy, and decides to drag it to the living room.

No one has budged. Maria places her chair opposite Ernest and Alice, who has closed her eyes and bowed her head. She's asleep. Anyway, she wouldn't have grasped a thing Maria told them because she doesn't understand French.

They don't ask any questions. The three merely look at her.

And she launches into her story.

She tells them the whole tale from start to finish. Her life during the past twelve years: Providence, her marriage, the disappearance of her husband, her heartbreaking separation from Rhéauna, Alice, and Béa, whom she'd had to send to live with their grandparents in Saskatchewan because she couldn't work in a cotton mill and bring up three girls at the same time – though that part they probably knew because their mother, Joséphine, had kept them informed during all those years while at the same time keeping her promise to Maria not to reveal where she was hiding – the arrival of Monsieur Rambert in her life when she had despaired of ever meeting another man, his kindness, politeness, his great generosity, the hope of a happy time when, finally, they realized their plan to bring her children to New England and start life over again, even if she was not officially a widow, an event she didn't deserve and that had come to her out of the blue. Then finally her second serious attempt to escape that she knows is illusory and pointless, that has brought her here to this stifling room, settled in like an outcast in front of a family court.

Not once does she lower her eyes. She keeps an eye on them all while she talks, looking from face to face, trying to guess what is hidden behind their gazes, but they let nothing show, except maybe Teena, whose eyes mist over when Maria talks about her pregnancy. She can count on one ally, then, who might perhaps defend her if the other two sentence her with no appeal.

All this time her sister-in-law Alice snores softly, her head resting on the back of the sofa, hands along her thighs, abandoned to soothing dreams, to the liberating numbness brought on by alcohol. Before the arrival of the damn migraine.

When she has finished, Maria closes her eyes, thinking to herself that she will only open them for their sentencing.

The first voice she hears is her brother's, but he is talking about his wife:

"I'll have to undress her and put her to bed. Sometimes I'd like to leave her there all night to shame her ..."

Then Tititte's:

"I'll help ..."

As nothing else is forthcoming, Maria opens her eyes again. Are they going to ignore what she's told them, forget what has been said, and pursue their conversation as if she weren't there in front of them, alone and desperate after that painful confession?

But Teena is kneeling down in front of her, moving her hands to lay them on her thighs. A plump and tiny little woman crouching on what was once a flowered carpet, threadbare now but clean. Her whole body is trembling and, when she speaks, Maria is obliged to bow her head to understand her sister.

"Me too, I had one ... A child ... A teeny-tiny baby ... With a man I wasn't married to ... and he left. His name is Ernest, like our brother, and he's the love of my life."

The other two are looking at the ground. Maria understands that they couldn't say anything before Teena spoke. Suddenly her heart feels lighter, a breath of hope goes to her head, stuns her for a moment. She opens her arms, holds her sister tight while a great cry of deliverance escapes from her chest. They are both crying, embracing. Tititte wipes a tear; Ernest, for his part, coughs into his fist.

Alice lets out a little laugh in her sleep; she is dreaming about angels or about a new bottle of Bols gin.

The sun is beating down on the back of her neck and it feels good. For several minutes Rhéauna has been sitting still on her wooden bench, waiting for her heart to slow down. Fear has finally left her, she's even decided to forget the incident with Monsieur Simoneau so her day won't be ruined before it's even ten o'clock. The main thing is, she got away from him. She'll think about all that another time. Now she is content to watch the passersby, in particular, the women strolling along St. Catherine Street chattering, ignoring the sound of traffic – more and more loud and chaotic. There are explosions of sounds all around her: horses neigh as if they're in pain; car horns honk for no reason; multiple streetcars travel on the pavement behind her bench, nearly touching her back, but not once does she turn around. It's the human crush that interests her. She could spend the whole day there in the sun, watching the parade of dresses in all colours, some to her amazement so short the entire laced boot is visible, unthinkable where she comes from. She'd love to sit there all morning, trying to catch snatches of conversation, laughing at the way some people walk, imagining that she's stroking babies' heads. Suddenly she remembers her ridiculous plan and she is swept away by a sense of obligation, the need to prove to herself she can do it. She's about to leave her daydreams behind and get up to start heading west when a fluty voice cries out her name. "Rh'auna D'rosiers! What are you doing all by yourself like you're lost? Waiting for your mother?"

It's Marie-Berthe Beauregard, the worst shrew, the clingiest girl in her class at school, now waddling over to her, accompanied by a very capable woman whom she resembles so much it's scary. They could be two versions of the same woman, one in the prime of life, nimble, bounding with energy, and seemingly proud of herself;

the other still being formed – a draft version, you might say – who does everything she can to look like the first one: same hair style, same gait but not so agile, head certainly not held in quite the same way. And the same tendency to stoutness. But it's mainly the faces that attract attention: they're identical, so much so that heads keep turning as they go by. Everyone seems to be waiting to tell them they look alike. As if the pair didn't know and hadn't expected to be noticed. Obviously with no success.

Rhéauna, alas, can't avoid them and stays seated, hands folded on her lap, annoyed with herself for not leaving sooner.

"Your mother go shopping?"

Marie-Berthe was one of the first pupils of the Académie Garneau to laugh at Rhéauna's accent, though she herself speaks with a very rough one herself, where the words, chewed up and distorted, are often hard to grasp. At least for Rhéauna, whose grandmother always insisted that she pronounce every word clearly and properly, maybe even overdoing it a little, but comprehensible. What difference does an accent make if two people understand each other?

"Me and my ma, we gotta buy boots for me to go to school in."

Rhéauna realizes then that Marie-Berthe is wearing their school uniform, a convent girl's black serge dress with a white celluloid collar and cuffs. In this heat! No wonder she's so red and shiny!

Rhéauna can't stop herself from looking her over from head to toe, saying, "How come you've got on that dress in the middle of August, for the love of God? We have to wear it all year, from September till June, isn't that enough?"

Marie-Berthe sits beside her and runs a finger between her stiff collar and her damp neck.

"I just told you, we're gonna buy me boots!"

"You have to wear your uniform to buy boots?"

"They have to go together!"

"Sure, but there aren't forty kinds of shoes for us. The sisters make us all wear the same ugly clodhoppers so we look like a bunch of old maids!"

Faced with Rhéauna's relentless argument, Marie-Berthe decides to change the subject, pointing to her classmate, telling her mother, "Look, ma, that's the one I told you talks funny."

Madame Beauregard brings her hand to her mouth as if to hold back a laugh. And gives Rhéauna a condescending look.

"I see what you mean."

Rhéauna wants to bite them.

"That there one, is it her that came all the way across Canada to be with her ma that's a widow?"

Madame Beauregard frowns, overdoing a compassionate look reminiscent of the expressions of movie actresses Rhéauna thinks are so ridiculous with their big, round eyes and their heavy makeup.

"Your ma's a widow? You poor child!"

Okay, enough. Rhéauna stands up and smooths her pretty red dress, turning around in front of Marie-Berthe, who goes on sweating in clothes too hot for the season.

"Excuse me but I have to buy train tickets to get back to Saskatchewan. I'm going with my widowed mother and my little orphan brother."

Marie-Berthe is startled.

"You're going?"

"Yup."

"Going back to Saplaschewan?"

"That's right. We'll never see each other again. Aren't you glad?"

Rhéauna strolls away and leaves them standing there.

She regrets it immediately. She suspects she won't actually be going away and she'll have to confront Marie-Berthe Beauregard, with her accent that you could cut with a knife, at the beginning of September; that she'll most likely take advantage of it to laugh even harder with her friends, each one more malevolent than the rest, who made her life impossible during her first year at that lousy Académie Garneau.

Before the school year had begun, though, she'd spent several days getting ready. Because she came from far away, she knew she spoke differently from the other children who were going to be her classmates and their reactions might not be the most positive. She'd had some trouble at first understanding certain Montrealers who, like Marie-Berthe Beauregard, spoke too fast and chewed half their words.

But what she had encountered at the Académie Garneau – mockery, nastiness, jealousy – was way worse than she'd expected. It's true that she hadn't helped her cause by revealing over the first few days how smart she was and how fast she learned. They might have tolerated her Saskatchewan accent, though it was slight, if she hadn't shown herself to be so brilliant. To be accepted by the other girls and to earn their respect, she'd worked tirelessly to make up for their obvious advance over her – the teaching system in Montreal was very different from the one in Maria, where all grades met in the same classroom and the teacher taught every subject to every level at the same time – and with the first report card of the year, the one in September, she'd come fourth in her class. Instead she should have done the opposite, played the little country girl, none too bright, lost in the big city, or acted insolent with the nun in order to attract the sympathy of the dunces in her class. Insolence and clumsiness would have brought respect. Instead, because of her academic success, twenty-four little girls had hated her because she'd got ahead of them in a few weeks and the three others had hated her because they felt threatened by her talents.

As well, the nun had taken a liking to her, or pity, and before long she was called brown nose and teacher's pet.

Condemned to mockery and shunned by the others, she still decided not to let herself be worn down by despondency and had thrown herself into schoolwork with a frenzy that very soon bore fruit: on the October report she had gone up one place. And made herself one more enemy.

The little girls who attended the Académie Garneau weren't fundamentally nasty. But they'd been raised by mothers who themselves had been brought up by mothers from a society too long closed in on itself, women who didn't trust anything different from what they knew – especially strangers – and who educated their children according to the strict principles of a stifling religion that abused the word *charity* without having the slightest idea what it was. It was because of ignorance, then, that her classmates had first lacked generosity towards this newcomer who didn't speak French the way they did, and then because of jealousy.

Rhéauna suffered it all, telling herself that her classmates would accept her eventually, appreciate her good qualities, when the accent that made her different from the others subsided and, in time, disappeared.

And meanwhile she has prepared herself for another difficult school year – though she'd noticed in the spring that at least one girl, Diane Derome, seemed to want to befriend her – with no hope of seeing her two sisters join her because her mother had soon stopped talking about the plan.

Rhéauna hadn't looked back even once to check whether the loathsome Marie-Berthe and her grotesque mother were following or if they'd turned at the corner of St. Hubert and St. Catherine to head for De Montigny in the north or Dorchester in the south. Or to see their expressions, wide-eyed and gape-mouthed after her last scathing remark.

She's well aware that she'll have to pay for her nasty words if she ever goes back to the Académie Garneau, that Marie-Berthe will waste no time telling about their meeting to anyone who'll listen and they will probably work even harder to keep her out of things. "You want nothing to do with us? Okay, play by yourself. Have fun!" But the opportunity was too fine to let go and it's true that she wanted nothing to do with Marie-Berthe Beauregard and her kind. Solitude accepted – though imposed – would perhaps be better in the end than the sarcasm and spitefulness of the previous year. A peace that would cost a lot, granted, but that could save her from plenty of anxiety.

She walks past the St. Jacques Church located just across from one of those nightclubs like the one where her mother works, a little farther away. Then she crosses St. Denis, which is even more congested than Amherst. As she looks at the pandemonium, she thinks that never in her life is she going to drive an automobile if ever women get the right: drive twenty miles an hour, avoid pedestrians, manoeuvre around horses, concentrate on the wheel, the levers, the pedals … Too complicated. She probably wouldn't have time to see what was going on around her. Store windows, strollers, the weather – real life. That's why people come to St. Catherine Street, not to run around like lunatics, seeing nothing of what's going on, overwhelmed by the smell of automobile exhaust and horse manure. Let's hear it for walking! Or public transportation. Even if it frightens her a little.

A streetcar comes along, sounding its warning *klang-klang-klang.* She could hop onto one at the next stop, it would be faster, she'd know sooner what to expect. For the rest of her life. No. She enjoys wandering aimlessly even if it means having unpleasant encounters – the one with Monsieur Simoneau and the one with Marie-Berthe Beauregard were both disagreeable – but a plan like hers, she thinks as she hurries towards St. Lawrence Boulevard, requires more than a simple trip across town to buy train tickets. When you're about to do something of such magnitude that it will transform your life and the lives of those around you, it takes a minimum of preparation, of reflection – doesn't it?

Exactly. She hasn't really thought – and reflected not at all – about what she'll do at Windsor Station now that she's left the house; rather, she has avoided thinking about it and has let her mind wander every time the idea came to her. To avoid having to face her own silliness, the absolute impossibility of carrying out such a plan? Yes. No doubt. (As a diversion again she looks at the houses with six or seven storeys she'd got used to so quickly after the first weeks of astonishment.) Basically, she doesn't want to think about all that – to reflect, go into it deeply, analyze. She wants to be content with the dreaming she can do for a few hours, for the excitement – and also for the beauty of it. It's a wonderful thing, it seems to her, to want to save your family from the war! She'll be able to say that she tried, that she wanted to help, that she'd done everything to make it happen. That beautiful dream. She knows she's repeating herself, that she has already thought it through several times since she left Montcalm Street, but she refuses to reflect any further. She may not save Jerusalem like the Crusaders in the novels she's tried to read, with violence so repellent she left them for the boys, but she too has set out on foot, has a long way to travel, and no doubt other adventures to live through before she arrives at the station. A cinema marquee rises above her. A gigantic sign, already lighted up at ten o'clock in the morning, announces: "Théâtre Français" and in smaller characters: "J.O. Hooley, manager." She raises her head, cranes her neck. In big black letters on a white background she reads: "*Quo Vadis* now playing for a second consecutive month. Eight reels, ten thousand feet of film, two hours and fifteen minutes of fascination. Two thousand seats for 5 or 10 cents." Next, the schedule: 12:30, 2:30, 4:30, 6:30, 8:30. Rhéauna scratches her head. How can a film that lasts for two hours and fifteen minutes start every two hours?

It all reminds her of something else but she can't remember what it is. Maybe a conversation she heard ... She approaches the photos. A lady with no clothes on, looking panicked, is tied to a post and a huge bull is threatening her with his horns. In the next photo a man, with no clothes either – all he has on is a short skirt and sandals with straps to his knees that show almost as much as when she changes her little brother's diaper – he is fighting a furious tiger. Farther away, poor people dressed in rags are flung into the arena to feed the lions ...

That's it, now she's found it. The poor Christians of Rome who are going away to be eaten raw! Her mother and her two aunts had talked about this film for the whole evening during one of their card parties.

So it was a poker game that brought them together again: Tititte, Teena, and Maria. They had decided to meet at Teena's place, a good-size apartment near Fullum Park in Plateau Mont-Royal. Ernest had excused himself once again "because Alice was under the weather." The three Desrosiers sisters weren't taken in, they knew perfectly well what that meant and had simply shrugged and replied, "Poor Ernest, he certainly doesn't deserve that."

It was Maria's night off at the club but she'd brought her two children: Théo had caught a summer cold, the most dangerous according to Maria's mother, Joséphine, who had terrified the children for years, watching out for the slightest symptoms of a cold during their summer holidays. "A cold in the winter, that's normal, it's freezing, you catch a cold from your feet and they're full of germs. But you get a cold in summer because the whole body is sick, the blood is rotten, and you can come down with all kinds of *pneumonies* without even noticing. You can't trust them, those summer *pneumonies*! Just say the word and you're dead!" She fed them things that were fattening and filling to keep them healthy, winter dishes she spent all day long preparing and desserts far too rich, saying things like: "Have a nice thick steak, that'll make new blood!" or "Nice thick cream's going to smother the germs!" For the Desrosiers children, even Ernest, it was now second nature to watch out for summer colds for fear of catching pneumonia, even if they'd been away from their mother and her ridiculous beliefs for ages. Maria didn't go so far as to stuff Rhéauna and Théo with fatty food all summer to kill germs as her mother had done, but she still panicked a little when Théo had started to cough in the middle of June.

Rhéauna was rocking her little brother, murmuring a nursery rhyme to put him to sleep, when the conversation around the table slipped towards a film the three Desrosiers sisters had just seen at the Théâtre Français. It had made an impression on them all.

Teena, the most romantic of the three, the quickest to shed tears over the woes of ZaSu Pitts or Lillian Gish, called it the most wonderful film she'd ever seen.

"I cried so much I could hardly see a thing in the last half-hour!"

The other two had laughed as they picked up the cards they'd just been dealt.

Tititte had coughed into her fist.

"I see now! You soaked our three hankies so when the girl was nearly gored by the bull I didn't have a thing to cry into!"

Maria flung her cards on the table, cursing her bad luck.

"I pass. As usual. Jeez, I have lousy luck at cards!"

She had lit a cigarette before the scandalized expressions of her sisters who still thought that any woman who dared to smoke, even in private, was vulgar. But after all, Maria worked in a nightclub amid drunks and hookers, they shouldn't be surprised if she had caught some of their bad habits. Maria had half-closed her eyes as she blew out her first puff of blue smoke.

"If you ask me, the guy who played Quo Vadis? I wouldn't have kicked him out of my bed!"

Tititte frowned.

"What do you mean, the guy who played Quo Vadis? Nobody in that movie's called *Quo Vadis*!"

Maria sipped some beer while she looked at her sister.

"We didn't see the same one, that's for sure. That guy, the good-looking one with the blond ringlets – he wasn't a Mister Vadis and his first name was Quo?"

After that, the conversation went off in all directions at once, so much so that Rhéauna couldn't remember who had said what, just that the argument had been lively and, as usual, nothing was settled because the three Desrosiers sisters had debated each on her own side, ignoring the arguments of the others.

"I can't remember his name, all I know is it was more complicated than Quo Vadis. Longer, anyway."

"Besides, they all had names nobody could say in that movie …"

"That's right, all those names were like parts of the Mass! I wouldn't be surprised if there was one called *Ite Missa Est*!"

"You're right about that … What was her name anyway, Proscula something …"

"The girls, they all had Latin names and the actors were all Italian."

"Yeah – and they weren't as good as Americans."

"But a lot better looking."

"No better looking than my handsome Henry Walthall. Not in a hundred years."

"You and your Henry Walthall."

"Have you ever seen a better-looking man than Henry Walthall? No? Then shut up!"

"We don't even know him."

"You always carry on about him and we don't even know who he is!"

"He's a big movie star."

"Maybe in the States, but not here."

"Here, you're a bunch of ignoramuses."

"We're ignorant because we don't know Henry Walthall? Don't make me laugh!"

"Didn't you see him in *The God Within* with Blanche Sweet a couple of years ago? He was so handsome I went to see it three times in the same week!"

"Good Lord, you didn't have much to do down in Providence!"

"Okay, girls, let's change the subject or we'll fight … Let's talk about the scenery … I can't get over it! They say in the papers that it's the biggest set ever built for a movie … That they built the whole city of Rome!"

"Don't exaggerate!"

"I'm telling you."

"My Lord, the whole city of Rome? That wouldn't fit in a studio!"

"It wasn't in a studio, it was outside! You could tell it was real sky and everything, not a painting, the trees were real trees …

Getting back to Quo Vadis, even if it wasn't his name, he looked good in his little skirt ..."

"I was a little bit shocked at first ..."

"Sure, but that's what everybody wore back in those days – little skirts."

"Our Lord didn't wear a little skirt!"

"Our Lord wasn't a Roman!"

"You mean the Romans wore little skirts and the Jews wore long dresses?"

"I guess so. The first Christians, they wore long dresses too. What were they called? Oh right, I remember – a tunic! That's what it's called, a tunic. In the movie all the first Christians wore tunics like Our Lord Jesus Christ!"

"Except the centurion."

"What centurion?"

"You know, the one who converted. The Roman? You'll never convince me his name was Centurion."

"That's what everybody called him."

"Sure, just like you're called Waitress when you're on the job. It doesn't mean your name is Waitress Desrosiers!"

"So centurion's a profession?"

"Yeah, he's a soldier. And he wasn't going to wear a tunic just because he'd converted!"

"Anyway, it's hard to believe the Romans really did dress like that but that's no reason to show us everything."

"We didn't see everything!"

"You didn't look properly ..."

"That's what *you* think ... If there's anyone who looked, it was me."

"We know that, you must be used to seeing men in little skirts where you work."

"There's no men in little skirts where I work! And anyway, what out of the blue have you got against where I work?"

"Girls, girls, that's not what we're talking about."

"That's true, we're talking about my handsome Quo Vadis!

"Quo Vadis wasn't his name!"

"If that's what I want to call him, it's my business!"

"Anyhow, when I saw the bull charging the girl, I think I leaned back three rows!"

"Yeah, and you ripped my hanky!"

"I did not!"

"No? Well, I had to throw it out when I got home."

"Me, it was Rome on fire that got me. Even though it wasn't in colour I could see the red fire! And it made me sit up and take notice."

"I understand, burning all that wonderful scenery! The whole city of Rome! Can't you just see it, setting fire to Montreal for a movie?"

"It wasn't the real city of Rome, you just said so yourself, it was only a set."

"I'd like to believe you but it was so realistic you'd think it was the real thing."

"That's why they make movies. So we think they're real."

"Well, they sure got me."

"Me too, 'specially with the short skirts."

"Doesn't mean he wasn't crazy, that Nero should've been locked up."

"Or set fire to Rome when he was playing the harp."

"Not a harp, it was a lyre."

"Listen, you, just because you went to London, you aren't going to teach us about musical instruments."

"But that's what was on the titles in between scenes, you could've read it."

"Anyway a harp, a lyre, what's the difference? We couldn't even hear it."

"Ah, so if you'd heard it you'd have known the difference. You think you're so smart ..."

"Girls, we've stopped playing cards."

A brief respite, just a few seconds, followed, then the argument came up again, worse than ever. But Rhéauna had stopped listening.

She'd closed her eyes and joined her little brother in sleep. Still, she'd dreamed about men in little skirts, and Rome burning.

🍍

Rhéauna smiles as she looks at the photos.

"Look, that must be him, Nero, the big fat man with a nasty expression, holding a lyre."

Smoke behind him. Rome on fire. It must smell like grilled meat! Yuck! She moves on to the next photo. A man, very handsome and muscular, holds a sword in one hand and a fishing net in the other. The Romans were fighting with fishing nets! Is that ever weird! But the actor is very handsome and she wonders if he's the one her mother had talked about during the last poker game. Who was right? Was his name Quo Vadis or not? *Vadis*, that sounds okay but *Quo*, really? That man's mother didn't have much imagination!

She wished she could get permission to see that movie. Several times she'd asked her mother, who told her it was a film for adults only and in any event she was too young to look at short little men and get an eyeful. *Eyeful?* That was a new word she thought was very interesting. An eyeful. How much could an eye socket hold? Or she could come in secret some afternoon, sacrifice five cents of her seven dollars and eleven cents, buy a cone at the nearby ice cream parlour, a lemonade too, and witness the massacre of the first Christians and see Rome on fire. For two whole hours and a quarter. In front of short little men like Quo Vadis and Jews in long dresses.

Dreaming is pointless, her money will have to go to something other than the movies. She heaves a sigh.

To her amazement, everything seems fine at the corner of St. Lawrence and St. Catherine, even though it's one of the busiest intersections in Montreal. There are lots of people, yes, and the many kinds of automobiles and streetcars make an infernal noise as they do everywhere else, but here at the moment it's all harmony. Maybe because of the traffic cop who's posted there all day long, who works his whistle and his hands with exemplary zeal and looks scathingly at all offenders. He is a respected man at whom everybody looks before they cross, pedestrians as much as drivers of cars, calèches, or streetcars. People wait for his signal before they move. And he seems to enjoy his position of power because his chin is lifted and his chest is inflated under a uniform that's too warm for the season.

Just as Rhéauna is about to cross St. Catherine Street and head south, he raises his arm, delivers an authoritative blast, takes his whistle out of his mouth, and starts to howl insults enough to give you the shivers, in a mixture of French and English that in other circumstances would be incomprehensible but that in these circumstances is absolutely clear. All heads turn towards the driver of a car who has dared to disregard the sign meaning *Stop* that the police officer has just given them. The officer strolls into the intersection, and even though traffic is blocked for a good minute, no one protests. Rhéauna listens to the policeman's invective and feels relief that she's no longer the victim; instead this poor driver is the target, and she watches him tie himself in knots with his head down and his shoulders hunched. After a loud, "And I don't want to see you at my intersection," in French, then a comical, "Don't come back, I don't want to see you *à mon intersection* anymore!" the policeman sticks his whistle back in his mouth and resumes his role. The driver squirms, he writhes, and everything goes on as if nothing had happened: a movie that had been stopped for a minute, then started up again with no warning. It was as if life, suspended for a moment, had waited for this signal before resuming its normal course.

Now that Rhéauna has heard things about the place where her mother works she has decided to go and see for herself what it looks like. It's a little farther down St. Lawrence, apparently, next to the Marché Saint-Laurent, one of the most wonderful markets in town, where there are foodstuffs so exotic you can't imagine that they're edible, and located just across from the Monument-National, an enormous theatre her mother claims is the most magnificent in the whole province of Quebec. Even though Maria has not set foot outside Montreal since her arrival two years earlier.

The store windows are covered with ads written in a language Rhéauna doesn't know. It looks a little like the tracks left by hens in the snow in winter in Saskatchewan. Maria has talked to her a lot about the Jews who live around the nightclub where she works, but she has never mentioned their writing. Curious, Rhéauna walks up to a store window. It's different from the signs she's seen in the Chinese laundry but just as complicated. It's funny to think there are people who understand what's written there while for her it's an unfathomable mystery. She understands nothing in Italian, Spanish, and little in English, but at least they use the same alphabet ... And what about those who write like that, do they understand *her* writing? She takes a closer look. It's like drawings. Do Jews write with drawings? Wouldn't that be wonderful! A whole way of writing made of drawings!

In the window are crowded all sorts of goods: rolls of fabric, rugs, knick-knacks, candlesticks, sets of extravagantly engraved sets of dishes that look like solid gold ... Like Ali Baba's cave.

An old woman emerges from the shop, looks at her, smiles, and says something that seems friendly but of course she can't understand.

She blushes to the roots of her hair and is annoyed at herself for not understanding. She knows it's absurd but she can't help it and eventually she murmurs a tiny little, "I can't understand what you're saying but thank you just the same!" before she turns her back on the old woman and runs away.

Silly fool, maybe the woman understands French, or English. Maybe she could have talked to her!

The crowd around the market is dense and noisy. Men announce to the assembled crowd, in several languages at once, products of all kinds from all over the world. The wooden stalls collapse under the weight of vegetables and fruits, most of them unknown to Rhéauna, wide-eyed at the sight of so many exotic foods. Some yellow things, plumper than bananas but that aren't, tower over cucumbers nearly monstrous in size; tomatoes in pretty pale pink, one of the only familiar things, rub shoulders with a huge round vegetable shaped like a green pumpkin. Can you eat that, a green pumpkin? Rhéauna walks up to it. Apparently the green ones are squashes; the long yellow ones, summer squashes. The signs are in French, in English, and in that weird writing of which she just studied a sample on the window of Ali Baba's cave. Farther away is a pyramid of a vegetable called *aubergine*, whose warm purple colour is thrilling. She knows the words *courgette* and *aubergine*, she's read them in books set far away, in Europe or Africa, she knows you can eat them, but it's the first time she's seen one. She goes up and down the aisles strewn with cabbage leaves and old heads of lettuce, looking at everything and breathing in as much as she can of the unknown smells all around her. She drowns in it, closing her eyes when it smells too good.

But where does it all come from? Where does it grow? Do all these people holding out their wares with a smile grow them, these vegetables she doesn't know because her mother lacks curiosity and falls back on those that are basics in her country's cooking: potatoes, turnips, carrots, cabbage, celery? What does this eggplant taste like? And what do you eat along with it? She would like to ask questions, ask if there are recipe books – sure there are, silly twit, but in what language? – take some money out of her pocket and buy that, there, or that strange fruit over there that's called a *pamplemousse*! Or do all these products come by train from countries to the south, sunny countries where there are oranges, lemons, pineapples, before they're offered here, at the Marché Saint-Laurent, to the people who know them and miss them because they don't grow in Canada? Ah, here's one she recognizes: a pineapple! She picks it up, it's covered with prickles as if it doesn't want to be touched and it's heavier than she'd imagined. She brings it to her nose and shuts her eyes.

She knows canned pineapple, she and her little brother are crazy about it and their mother gives them some now and then, when they've been good, but the smell of the fruit itself is more subtle, less pronounced. Her mouth is watering and she realizes she's hungry. How do you eat it? You can't bite into it; after all, it isn't a pear or an apple! You have to peel it, take out the core or the pit if there is one, cut it into round slices like the ones in the cans. It's too big, it would never fit in a can. Does that mean that the ones in cans are baby pineapples? Is it complicated to grow them? And do they have seeds like apples or oranges?

When she opens her eyes a big, jovial man with his hands on his hips is looking at her and smiling. He says a few words to her, maybe in that language written with drawings, and she replies that she only speaks French. He shrugs – he can't understand her either! He leans across his stall and takes out a plate laden with thick slices of fresh pineapple. He picks one up with his pudgy fingers and offers it to Rhéauna, who doesn't know if she should accept it. She hears her mother telling her once again not to speak to strangers, not to accept anything from them, to run away as fast as she can if they're too nice. She also thinks about Monsieur Simoneau, who treated her like a thief or at least pretended to. Is this fruit seller a Big Bad Wolf more hypocritical than that other man and does he seduce his victims with pineapple slices? But how can she resist a slice of pineapple? She looks around. Nothing could happen to her in the middle of this crowd, in the middle of the market, as exotic and strange as it is.

She holds out her hand, already mad at herself for her weakness of character.

It explodes immediately in her mouth, it's both sugary and tart, her tongue is burning, it stings and tickles at the same time, it's hot, it grates – and it's delicious. And you can feel it all the way to your nose. It's not as sweet as what you find in cans, but it's better! Her expression is happy and tears stand out in her eyes.

The fat man looks as if he's going to ask her if she likes it.

She swallows her first mouthful, smiles.

"It's better than good, it's delicious! It's fantastic! It's wonderful!"

She calls on the longest adjectives she knows and only rarely uses in ordinary conversations. And she savours them nearly as much as the mouthful of fruit she's just swallowed.

The man gestures to let her know that he can understand the gist of what she said even if he doesn't understand the words, and again Rhéauna bites into the slice of pineapple.

The second mouthful is very different from the first, milder, less invasive, and she chews for a very long time to extract all the juice from the pulp and to make her pleasure last. It's stringy, it gets stuck between her teeth, but it's good to the very last bite! And sweeter and sweeter.

Just as she's about to swallow, a very distant memory comes back. She has eaten it before. A slice of pineapple. Once. In Maria. Now she remembers that Grandma Joséphine come back from Monsieur Connells's general store with that thing covered with prickles, a fruit rare in Saskatchewan, which she'd served with ice cream, telling her husband and granddaughters they might never see it again in their little village. Rhéauna hadn't liked it, she'd found it too acid, and her grandmother had looked disappointed.

She apologizes to Grandma Joséphine as she finishes her slice of pineapple and swears she'll think of her whenever she eats it.

"To your health, Grandma. Maybe this is the only one you'll ever eat."

For a fraction of a second she thinks she might never eat one again if she goes back to Saskatchewan.

She licks her hand. The fat man laughs, hands her a damp rag with which she wipes her face. She wonders if her hand will be sticky for the rest of the day. She thanks him even though she knows he doesn't get a word she says, waves goodbye, and keeps walking up and down the fragrant aisles of the Marché Saint-Laurent.

A saleswoman who speaks French with a strange accent – she rolls her *R*s even more than Montrealers – tells her she looks lovely in her pretty red dress and gives her an orange. Rhéauna peels it and eats it while she explores the whole market. Two fresh fruits in a row, what luck! She spends the next fifteen minutes on the lookout for fruits and vegetables she doesn't know, in ecstasy over the beauty of their names as much as their shapes and varied colours. When she has walked around the entire market, stunned by everything she's seen and heard, and ends up on the sidewalk outside, across St. Lawrence Boulevard from the Monument-National, she realizes that she'd forgotten the goal of her venture onto this street – and even her intention of going all the way to Windsor Station – so much of what she's seen has fascinated her, and she hurries to the left in the hope of spotting the nightclub where her mother works. It's called Paradise, it shouldn't be hard to find.

It's a rundown building in red brick and grey stone near the corner of Dorchester. At night with the signs lit up, the people walking around, the music that bursts out when the door is opened, it may not be so depressing. In daytime, though, it looks like a house abandoned long ago. Maybe because the windows, not very clean, are hung with heavy drapes of no particular colour that suggest neglect and sloppiness. And because the door, which is made of solid oak reinforced with metal, looks like the one in a storybook prison. You would say that it's closed for good and that the small notice advertising *"Rita Rouleau, chanteuse à voix"* dates from another age, left behind in the rush to leave the place.

Rhéauna tries to picture her mother walking through the doorway of this place, spending hours there every night serving alcoholic drinks to noisy couples who aren't always listening to the performers onstage – it was Maria who told her that – making her way among the tables in her black-and-white striped dress, the uniform of Paradise waitresses, leaving long after midnight, going down Dorchester at a good clip on her way home. She doesn't go home. That woman isn't the same person as her mother. And she has just a few minutes, between St. Lawrence Boulevard and Montcalm Street, to become again the Maria Desrosiers she has learned again how to love in the past year. She is well acquainted with the daytime version of her mother, but totally ignorant of the one she becomes at night.

She thinks to herself that she has gone too far, she should have stayed ignorant, not come to stand in front of the building at an hour when it seems so depressing. She should have gone back onto St. Catherine Street as soon as she'd left the Marché Saint-Laurent and run west, towards Windsor Station, towards her dream of freedom. What stands in front of her now is reality, totally naked and not very pretty. While in her head is a fine dream that helps her get through life. Does her mother have a dream that helps her? When she gets up in the morning, exhausted, especially when Rhéauna leaves for school and Maria has to take care of Théo, what is she thinking about? Dreaming about? She has never lingered there. This is the first time she has thought about her mother in this way and she stands there planted in front of the Paradise with a new image of Maria engraved on her heart. She is struck by a thought: if her mother has stopped talking about bringing Alice and Béa from Saskatchewan it's because life would be impossible, not because she has lost interest in her children. That revelation shakes Rhéauna entirely, to the point that she has to lean against the wall of the Paradise. A dizzy spell overcomes her when the thought that it's not from the war that she has to save her mother and Théo, it's from the hopeless life here, in Montreal … And if she doesn't take responsibility for reuniting her family, it will never happen.

"My story's pretty ordinary. It's been around since Creation. Ever since men have been tricking women, ever since women have chosen to believe them. But just because it's ordinary, it can still be sad."

Teena looks at each of them in turn as they sit gathered around her, listening. Tititte, her older sister who has heard the story countless times, is looking around vacantly. She has turned her head towards the living-room window and is gazing absently at the deserted street where there's no traffic, no pedestrians strolling, where nothing is happening. As for Ernest, he is looking down at his knees where his hands lie side-by-side; he could be studying his fingernails. It's obvious that he has no interest in listening yet again to this story that still seems to shock him. As for Alice, she left a while ago to go to bed, claiming a headache that everyone believed because with all she drank … (Anyway, she's never understood what is said and what happens in this family of fools of which she has married the one reasonable and easily manipulated member, but who allows himself to get involved in the not-always-clear doings of his sisters. She is convinced that this latest arrival, Maria, who'd disappeared into New England twelve years earlier, will be another example of a life irremediably ruined, maybe the worst of them all, that she has brought along her own share of hard-to-manage ordeals, calamities – a pregnant widow, maybe not a widow at all – penniless, jobless – Alice considers herself lucky to have good old Bols gin for an ally. The only one. But very reliable. Consolation in the face of the loneliness of a female Anglophone lost in a group of Desrosiers who refuse to live otherwise than in French, in the middle of a city where money belongs to the Anglos.)

Only Maria turns to look at her sister again. She wants a detailed account of everything Teena has lived through. Her revelation provided Maria the hope she needed: if Teena has had a child here in Montreal without being married, Maria herself will probably be able to impose her status of widow and not be rejected by those in this Catholic society who are even more intolerant, so she's heard, than those in Providence.

Teena goes on in her alto voice ... She now speaks for just the two of them: Tititte and Ernest are lost in their thoughts and are no longer listening.

"I was stunned like any woman by fine promises and good looks. Too handsome for me, I should have realized. Too shrewd, also. Too gentle. But love can't be ordered, can it? And I fell into it head first. He was as tall as I am short, he was as strong as a bear but at the same time as gentle as a lamb, and if his promises weren't original, they were precise and tempting enough for me to hang onto and I ... and I succumbed. That's a funny word, *succumb*. A word that makes you ashamed afterwards, and ugly, but it's so different when it's happening! If you succumb when you're not married, you're scared before, you're ashamed after, but if you're in love it's so glorious during! Especially if you're over twenty-five and still unmarried, when you're considered to be an old maid with no future because you're nearing your thirties and you never thought it could happen to you. You think it's all true. That it has arrived. Love. To succumb in advance when you're in love doesn't matter because you're sure it will be like that always, that it will be repeated an infinite number of times, the handsome hunk will stay handsome, the promises will stay the same, the traditional proposal will come sooner or later, the future is full of wonderful things that will make you forget everything unpleasant you've lived through to date. And ..."

She brings her hand to her heart, take a deep breath, fans her face with the other hand because she is blushing and can't control it.

"I don't know ... eventually you realize that things have changed a little, you see more and more differences between before you succumbed and after ... He had what he wanted, he's already looking for a way out, to get rid of you, he's a man,

they're all alike but you don't know that yet … You understand, you're dreaming about marriage again, and a family, and
happiness … It's stupid enough for tears, you never should've
believed you'd have that life because you think you're an intelligent woman, because your mother warned you, because your
father always kept an eye on the boys you went out with when
you were younger … But they're far away, they aren't there to
protect you, you wanted to run away from them, you're all alone.
And then you think you've hit the jackpot. That you'll be able
to hold your chin up in front of your parents when you see them
again, tell them, Look, you had nothing to be scared of, I'm
happy and I found that happiness by myself, I chose it by myself.
Until you realize one day you've been sick every morning for a
while now, that your handsome hunk gives you a funny look
when he finds you crouching in the bathroom, then something
terrible occurs to you. Finally you face facts, you see a doctor
who confirms the 'bad' news. And by the time you get home
again your handsome hunk isn't there. All that's left of him is a
shaving brush and a bowl of shaving soap. You knew it. All that
time you knew but you refused to see. You bawl when you smell
the shaving soap, you want to keep at least that part of him, his
smell, the smell of a clean gentleman besides … You don't try to
see him again either because you're too proud. You could make
him marry you, force him to face up to his obligations, but you
realize that the sight of him makes you sick, that you never want
to lay eyes on him again, you'd rather be banished from society
than be obliged to put up with his face for the rest of your life.
For the wrong reasons, besides. He never wanted marriage, not
him. And you don't want it either, oh no! Then just when you
think you've hit bottom, when you think you can't sink any deeper
into depression, someone suggests you go to see the nuns at the
Misericord Hospital, they'll know what to do, they'll help you,
protect you … But all they want … the only thing those goddamn
Sisters of Mercy want – at least that's how I understand it – is
to separate you from your child, take it away to give to someone

else, to a 'responsible' family who'll give it a roof, food, love –
as if you wouldn't be capable of loving your own child! They're
mean to you because you're a sinner, it's always your fault, never
the father's, they treat you like the worst of the hookers, they say
they'll let you into their hospital out of charity, but you suspect
the price you'll have to pay, the humiliation, the separation, the
loneliness when it's all over and you end up on the street ready
for the first handsome man you run into ... It's not us who ought
to be punished like that ... it's men! They're the ones, Maria,
with their fine speeches and their goddamn promises they never
intend to keep! I know I'm exaggerating, I know some are okay
but why is it always other women who encounter them? Take our
sister Tititte, who went all the way to England to find happiness
and came home practically running because her husband wasn't
what she thought ... Take you, who don't dare tell your Monsieur
Rambert you're expecting his baby because you're afraid he'll
leave you high and dry like they all do ... Is that fair?"

Teena takes Maria's hand in hers, squeezes till it hurts.

"I said to myself I'd never bring my child into the world in that
hospital and d'you know what I did? I went away. I left Montreal.
Like you've just left Providence. Another Desrosiers moving to
change her life! I took my suitcase, then I buried myself deep in
the Laurentians, in a little village in the middle of nowhere called
Duhamel where our cousin Rose, I don't know if you remember
her, married an Indian who settled her in a cabin with a dirt floor
on the shore of Long Lake. She found it, she found real love, but
you ought to see what it cost her! Understand? It's no better when
you find the real thing, when you find your great love."

She wipes a tear with an already-wet handkerchief.

"I talk a lot, don't I? But it does me so much good. If you only
knew ..."

She takes a deep breath, closes her eyes. She's come to the crux
of her story and she has to choose her words carefully.

"I left Montreal less than nothing, a fallen woman no one
would ever have wanted to take care of except those perverted

nuns – and all they wanted was to steal my baby; then I turned up in Duhamel a widow, like you are here, with a past I'd made up for myself during the train journey and a cousin who'd lie to protect me. After I'd promised some money, needless to say ... I'd kept my name, it was simpler, I said that my husband, a Monsieur Desrosiers also from Saskatchewan, had died peacefully and now I was looking for a house where I could retire for a while – the period of my widowhood – and then give birth to a child. Everyone believed me! I spent the winter buried under fifteen feet of snow, I celebrated Christmas with everybody, the curé even welcomed me from the pulpit because it's unusual for Montrealers to settle in Duhamel for any longer than hunting season, I baked apple pies, tourtières – can't you just see me, pregnant to the eyeballs, making tourtières? – I attended the little chapel with everybody else so I wouldn't stand out, I ran into deer in the middle of the village, I even fed them apples when the severe cold struck ... I melted into Duhamel ... No questions from anybody, never, even the village doctor and the midwife were discreet. They may have suspected something but they didn't say a word. I got heavier before their eyes, the baby would be there soon ... And what would become of me when he arrived? The only thing I know how to do is sell shoes. I don't have to tell you there's no shoe store in Duhamel ... You have to go to Papineauville to find one, I think ... So anyway I really did look for a house. Crazy, isn't it? The last thing I intended to do was stay in Duhamel but there I was looking for a house! The one I found, because I did find one, belonged to a brother and sister who were bringing up a child, a little boy. Scandal mongers said it was their own, a child of incest, but they claimed he was their little brother, their mother had died giving birth, I'm not sure exactly ... They needed money because they were moving to the city. She didn't look very happy, she seemed to want to hold on to their house, but he was one of those dreamers who wanted to look for his fortune in town by playing his fiddle, as if Montreal needed fiddlers ... Maybe he wanted to hide their sin in Montreal while I'd come to hide mine in Duhamel ... Anyway ... I got the house and all the land around it for peanuts. Even me, a poor saleslady in a shoe store, I was able to buy it all because their price was so low. They left in the middle of the night. We never heard a word from them ... I don't know if they're happy in Montreal. With their Gabriel. I just remembered the little boy's name: Gabriel. Anyway ... It was a nice house, not big, at the top of a hill, resting against a mountain that belonged to me and that I might sell part of to the Edwards Company that keeps making offers because they need the lumber to build who knows what ... Down below the forest company trains go by every morning ... There's no hydro, no running water, you have to go to the toilet outside, it's in the middle of the woods but it's so beautiful! Maybe that's because it's where I gave birth to my child, that could be, but every time I go back there – I'll have to take you one of these days, maybe you should give birth there too – every time I go there my appetite for life comes back. Two or three days of fresh air and cuddling my child and I'm ready to take on the world! Yes, I left him there, I didn't let the Sisters of Mercy give him away, I was the one to chose a family of farmers who love him and let me see him whenever I want. And then one of these days when I can afford it ... when we sell off part of the land ... especially when I work up the courage ... I'll bring him here to Montreal and I'll show him off to everybody. A love child? Hardly! A child of sin? So? He's *my* child! I've got the right to keep him for myself, don't I? But if he stays there, if he becomes a farmer like the ones who take care of him, I may go to Duhamel for the rest of my days, you never know ..."

She wipes a tear, blows her nose. Tititte is still looking out the window, Ernest hasn't budged either. "You know what it's like to be separated from your children ... I don't know how you manage, I see mine several times a year, and it's hard ... You, it's been years you haven't seen yours ... But at least you won't have the same trouble I had with mine, seems like you're a widow for real now ... If you've been telling the truth ... Nobody's going to force you to give up your child, they'll all feel sorry for you, they'll all want to lend a hand. The rest of us too, for sure. Not just Ernest, me and Tititte too. We'll try and find you a half-decent apartment, a half-decent job – at least if you can go on working, you're our sister, we won't leave you out on the street! Afterwards, after that we'll see. Meanwhile, you can sleep at our place ... There's no room here and Alice isn't always a barrel of laughs ... I've got a sofa in the living room, it's better than nothing."

The confidences over, she uses her hanky one last time before putting it in her purse, smooths her hair with her hand, straightens her skirt, manages to produce what could pass for a sad smile.

"This is quite a surprise, Maria. I don't know if we understand exactly what's just happened to us, it's like we're stunned, all three of us ... Maybe we'll realize what it all means, we'll be able to show you more affection. Right now we're so out of it we don't know if we're happy or not ... I guess maybe we are but it's like we don't know yet ... Well, I'm talking for myself. I don't know about the others."

Tititte turns towards them.

"Me, I know that I'm happy."

She can't add anything more. Standing, she bends over her sister and throws her arms around her.

"Welcome, little sister. It's going to be tough but we'll get there."

Ernest has looked up. "One more problem ... Go on, keep them coming, we can handle all your problems!"

His three sisters, who don't know if he's serious or kidding, decide that it's a joke. Again, a timid little laugh, very brief, a defeatist laugh that contains as much sorrow as amusement. They laugh without looking at one another, as if they are ashamed, while Ernest lights one of his damned Peg Top cigars that stink of vanilla.

A kind of discomfort settles into the front room. Confidences have been exchanged, help offered to someone who needs it, but they're all too tired, or troubled, to try reviving a conversation that's run out of steam, and a ponderous silence settles over the room.

They have to get up, call a taxi, don again the hats left on the bed, pull on gloves, kiss Ernest while saying goodbye. Though no one moves. When someone speaks it's to utter a cliché, state an obvious fact, winter's on the way, the leaves are all down, the aroma of fruit chutney, Alice's specialty, that will drift through the house for days. Nothing important is expressed. Someone has to put an end to this evening, all four know that, but it is quite apparent they don't know how and so let it drag on and on.

After a nearly unbearably long silence, Maria coughs into her fist and stares at her brother and sisters one after the other.

"Still, it's been twelve years since we've seen one another."

Is it the absence of their brother, who in any case has always laughed at their outpourings and at what he called their girly reactions, or is it the certainty they won't have to put up with the sarcasm of a male for whom any emotion is a sign of weakness? The fact remains that as soon as they're on the backseat of the taxi they push aside the stupid modesty that so far has prevented them from communicating as they would have liked. Tititte and Teena throw themselves into their sister's arms, hugging, hats in disarray, cries of joy rise into the icy night of Ville-Émard. Forgotten are Teena's deeply moving confession and Maria's sad story, the mood now is one of rejoicing. They are all fifteen years old again, with tons of anecdotes to share, all three at the same time, amid little girls' hysterical giggling, interrupted by exclamations and slapping thighs. The Desrosiers sisters are together again after being apart for twelve years and nothing, not even the taxi driver's mocking smile, can stop them from displaying their happiness.

Tititte and Teena decide to take the next day off after the latter suggests finishing the evening at her place with the dregs of a bottle of cognac she's been saving for a grand occasion.

"If this isn't a grand occasion I wonder what could be one! And you'll stay overnight too, Tititte. We'll do like we did when we were kids and we hid from Mama to tell one another love stories ..."

And so Maria's first night in Montreal ends in the euphoria produced by the uncensored revelations of three young girls who'd held back far too long and who now expressed unconstrained beauty and ugliness, good and bad. They realize they have more than negative things to talk about, that there have been good moments in their lives, they laugh at men, at themselves. They talk about Montreal, about Providence and London, about human beings, especially men who are the same everywhere, that is, unreliable and hypocritical; they give vent to the deceits of love, the price to pay, which is always too high, the abandonment found so often at the end of the road, the loneliness.

They stay up late, slightly tipsy towards the end, their remarks not so clear. They ramble on, saying they are rambling and laughing because they are still rambling. It's a night that is round, smooth, full, complete.

Tititte sleeps on the living-room sofa; Maria, with Teena. The eldest falls asleep quickly; you can hear her snoring at the other end of the apartment, while the remaining two keep chattering. They embrace each other as they had when one of the two was unhappy back home, so far away, so long ago, so very long ago, and they cry.

She has no more time to waste. Her mother told her that she had to be home by noon and it's already half-past ten. She'll have to keep a little money to take the streetcar back from Windsor Station or she'll be late. Again she takes the north side of St. Catherine Street going west to take advantage of the sun. Clouds are gathering above Mount Royal, heralding one of those August storms that catch you by surprise and leave you soaking wet in seconds. The sun will disappear any minute now. As long as it doesn't rain before she gets to Windsor Street. She should also be checking the names of the streets, she may be nearly there … She asks an old lady who tells her that she has a good dozen streets to cross, that it's over there, past Morgan's, past Eaton's.

"But start watching the street names when you get to Eaton's, it won't be far, maybe just a couple of blocks."

Just before she reaches St. Urbain Street, she goes past the Gayety, according to her mother a disreputable spot, where women take off their clothes for money. They go onstage in beautiful costumes and instead of singing or dancing … they take off their clothes! Men sit as if they were at the theatre and, far from watching the show in silence, they make a mighty noise as they suck cigars while the women undress. Rhéauna would be inclined to cross the street to study the posters, but time is short and she's content to read the title of the revue on the marquee that looks like a carbon copy of the one on the Théâtre Français where *Quo Vadis* is showing. It's called *Gay New Yorkers* and it stars Dolly and Stella Morissey. Sisters who get undressed? Maybe even together? Maybe they're even twins? Head filled with ladies in underwear crossing across the stage doing nothing but take off what's still on their bodies, Rhéauna quickens her pace, crosses Jeanne-Mance, then Bleury, careful to avoid looking at store windows she passes even though some seem very interesting.

She has been in unknown territory ever since she passed St. Lawrence. Suddenly everything looks more serious, the buildings are tall, the stone dark, the boutiques chic, no one is speaking French now, even people's physical appearance has changed. Or at least the way they move. Unlike those she met in the east end, these people seem not to be walking for the sake of walking, but to get somewhere – a little like Maria, who's not interested in the passersby – and would probably go so far as to jostle you if you didn't take care to avoid them when they made a beeline for you. Or maybe it's just an impression because she's in a part of the city she doesn't know. Oh, her mother has taken her to see the English *Père Noël* at Eaton's after showing her the French one at Dupuis Frères, but they rarely cross St. Lawrence because they know that the west end of Montreal belongs to *them*, to the Anglos who have money and who run everything, industries as much as businesses.

Once they're past Morgan's department store, where she has never set foot because her mother says that everything there costs too much, across from an odd-looking church that looks more like a fortified castle than a place of prayer – novels of chivalry again, Arthur, Merlin, Morgana, the dragons – Rhéauna comes to a halt in front of a magnificent grey tomcat, grey from his front claws to the tip of his tail, except for a triangle of white as a jabot that he seems to wear with great pride. He has seen her approach and has positioned himself along the way. He rubs his head against her boots, his muzzle on her stockings, purrs. She bends down, scratches him behind the ears. He stretches his head towards her, shuts his eyes for a moment. His purring becomes almost vehement.

"Pretty kitty! Yes, you're a pretty kitty! You're such a good kitty cat!"

He plunks himself down, looks up, stares her straight in the eyes. Or so she thinks.

"What're you doing all by yourself in the middle of St. Catherine Street? Are you lost? Are you? Are you lost?"

She looks around.

"Poor kitty cat, where on earth have you come from, so nice and clean, I bet you don't live on the street! Maybe you're the curé's cat. Is that it? Do you belong to the curé?"

She looks for the presbytery, which must be somewhere behind the church. She doesn't even know if it's a Catholic church. What if she's in a Protestant parish? In front of one of those churches where any depiction of God or his saints is forbidden, only geometrical motifs are allowed, a stern place where it's hard to dream. She likes to let her mind wander under the illustrated vault of her parish church and she often wonders what she would do during the curé's deadly dull sermons if she didn't have the richly coloured paintings and the gilded statues to look at. But who knows? Maybe Protestant sermons aren't as boring as Catholic ones.

"Maybe I should take you home?"

She looks at the jewellery store clock on the other side of St. Catherine Street.

"But I haven't got time … I feel bad, kitty, but I haven't got time to look after you."

She picks him up, walks to University Street, sets him down.

"Look, over there. That's where you live, over there."

He sits down again, looking up at her. And produces the most heartbreaking meow she's ever heard. It's not the meowing of an adult cat but that of a baby that's just lost its mother and now wants to nurse, a thin and pitiful sound that begins with a gulp and ends on a long, stifled note. Like a human sob. It's as if he were calling for help, as if he'll die in the next few minutes unless she acts now.

"My Lord, what kind of voice is that, you poor thing! Are you sick, kitty, is that it, you're sick?"

She hears her mother criticizing her yet again for spending too much time on stray animals, her strict warnings about dirt and disease. "You don't know where those animals have been, what they might have caught, what they're carrying in their fur …" Rhéauna steps back. Maybe the cat's not as clean as she thought. Or is suffering from a serious disease he could pass on to her?

No, he's too pretty, so pitiful with that little voice emerging from such a big body.

"It upsets me to leave you all alone like this but there's something really, really important I have to do … Go home, look, it's just behind the church … There's a yummy meal ready for you … Luscious leftovers. Or a mouth-watering box of canned food, maybe even Paris Pâté."

He doesn't budge. Nor does she.

She knows she's wasting precious time but she can't abandon this poor lost cat who seems to have become attached to her.

Her mother, again:

"Animals haven't got feelings, Nana, especially cats. They'll do anything for a free meal! I know, because there are enough of them prowling around the Marché Saint-Laurent and the trash cans in Paradise!"

This one, though, seems to really like her.

She shrugs. Silly girl! Two minutes ago he didn't even know her, how could he like her now?

She's heard about love at first sight. Her mother told her the story of Romeo and Juliet and took advantage of it to warn her to be careful about having feelings for two-legged cats who're too good-looking, too sharp, who often hide things that aren't very clean. Rhéauna had replied that if she were careful about animals with four legs and others with two she'd end up all alone in a corner, never talking to anyone – and nearly got a swat on her behind.

"Gotta go now, kitty cat – bye."

She crosses University Street, weaving through the cars.

When she is alongside Eaton's department store she has a fit of weakness that makes her turn around.

He is still there, sitting next to the fence around the church. She feels as if he's looking for her. Which is untrue of course, impossible. She stands on tiptoe to peer over a car that has just stopped in front of her. The cat is still there. Oh Lord, is he craning his neck the way she is, is he really looking for her? Has she just found a true friend, a companion with invincible love, with unwavering devotion, whom she has no right to abandon?

But what would she do with a cat if she leaves for Saskatchewan soon? Especially with a mother who doesn't want animals in her house? Hide him? Where? Feed him? How?

And during the next two minutes she experiences a tremendous wave of love. The whole time. From beginning to end. After the initial burst of love comes the certainty that she won't be able to live without him. No matter what it costs. She loves him too much, so much that it hurts. She'll hide him if she has to, she'll feed him table scraps after she settles him in the shed behind the house where her mother never sets foot. She'll set up a litter box that she'll change as often as possible, she'll give him a wool blanket for the coldest nights … She can't just leave him there at the corner of University and St. Catherine, he needs her and she needs him. Once again she's forgotten her plan for escape, she's even thought about the winter to come as if she were going to stay in Montreal, and concentrates on the chivalrous gesture of coming to the aid of a poor grey cat. She thinks she's brave, admires herself, is entertained.

She keeps watching him. He's washing himself, ears flat as if he were afraid, looking up now and then to see if she has come back, startled whenever a pedestrian comes too close … Then, gradually, her common sense returns, her heart regains its normal rhythm. Rhéauna tells herself that the curé can take better care of him because they know each other well, the grey kitty has a home, he's used to it, he's undoubtedly happy there. She thinks he's beautiful, yes, she would gladly kidnap him to keep him a prisoner of her love and her caresses, but his existence couldn't be hidden for very long and the price paid would be too high, for him as well as for her.

Finally, would he be happy with her? And for how long?

Most likely Théo wouldn't be able to keep it hidden either. A one-year-old child is nosy, demonstrative, he can't keep secret that there's a cat in the shed.

To think that at first she had hated this child who'd fallen into her life quite unexpectedly, a bundle of diapers, squalling and squirming, that she'd have gladly thrown him out the window in the beginning because he was responsible for her separation from her sisters and her grandparents. He'd won her over finally with his devastating smile, his bubbly laughter, his babbling that was so comical. He'd quickly become the focal point of her new life, her reason for existing. To accept the strange road her life had taken – a new city, too big for her, too far from home, a mother she didn't recognize, a school where she didn't feel accepted – she had concentrated on her burgeoning love for him; on the tickles she inflicted on him when Maria left for work in the evening and she was playing mother with him because that had been her role since she'd arrived from Saskatchewan; the baths she'd given him in a basin of warm water that made a terrible mess in the kitchen; and even his diapers, though disgusting, because she loved his gurgling when she powdered his bottom and his little wee-wee.

And most of all, the blessed moment when she put him into his bed and told him stories that he didn't understand but seemed to be listening to because he liked the sound of her voice. She often read his favourite part of *Alice in Wonderland,* the chapter about the hypocritical walrus and the oh-so-naive oysters that always made him chortle and Théo seemed to be listening, stirring the air with his tiny feet, playing with his toes, sucking his thumb, then he'd fall asleep with no warning, as if she'd knocked him out. Or bored him.

After all, hadn't his first word been *Auna,* not *Mama*? She hadn't dared tell her mother, she had even maintained that his very first word sounded like *Mama,* which thrilled Maria. Even if his first word had been *Mama,* wouldn't Rhéauna have assumed it was meant for her?

She'd have to choose between two loves then, one permanent, the other brand new and no doubt difficult. And most important, fleeting.

She heaves a long sigh, peers at the sky, which has darkened over again. Quickly turns around, starts running before it begins to rain – forget that beautiful grey animal, leave him to his fate as a stray cat, or one that's spoiled by a curé in need of affection – and find Windsor Street and the station.

The windows at Eaton's seem magnificent, already displaying autumn colours, but she doesn't linger; on the contrary she walks faster and peers at the name of every street she comes to. She even begins to despair of ever finding Windsor Station, considers asking for directions when she finds herself in front of Ogilvy's department store where her aunt Tititte works. She could go in and ask her! But how could she explain her presence so far west in the city? All by herself besides. After all, she can't confess her plan. One phone call and it would be all over.

She'll find an explanation.

If it were possible, she would say that the smells that bombard her when she pushes open the heavy door are even headier, more powerful than at Dupuis Frères. Maybe a little heavy because the store is smaller, but you would still want to drown in them forever and to smell nothing else for the rest of your life. The perfume counters glitter under the electric lights, the saleswomen stand even straighter and in fact there are more of them, even though there are fewer customers walking the aisles.

She has no idea where the glove counter could be.

She walks up to a tall string bean with a superior air and asks her. The woman doesn't even lower her gaze to answer.

"I'm sorry, I don't speak French."

Unable to formulate her request clearly and precisely in English, Rhéauna brings out the keyword which, fortunately, she knows: "Gloves!"

The saleswoman points towards the door through which Rhéauna has just entered. She'd walked past it without realizing! She retraces her steps and cranes her neck.

In the southeast corner of the store, behind a solid counter of carved wood, is her aunt Tititte, more impressive than when she comes to play cards with her sisters. Her violet dress, severe and indescribably chic, makes her look a little older but that's not serious. It may even be intentional. Buying gloves, the final touch on an elegant outfit, is an important act and the woman who sells them to you must radiate as much experience as devotion.

As it happens, Tititte Desrosiers is showing gloves to an old lady who holds herself very erect despite her advanced age. Tititte speaks gently to her, it seems, she takes each glove, strokes it, praises its beauty and softness, the fine seams, the delicacy of the leather. All quite graciously, while retaining her dignity and even a certain nobility. A queen addressing another queen. Her bearing is even more noble than that of her customer.

Rhéauna is fascinated. This saleswoman is nothing like the mother's sister she knows, so comical and so light in her movements, so sad at times too though she never says why, to the point that you would want to hug her and tell her it doesn't matter, it will pass. At times like those, Maria calls her Sister Nostalgia or Sister Blue. On the contrary, the person across from Rhéauna is an impressive woman who oozes confidence, of whom no one would ever think that she might have moments of weakness. How can someone transform herself so completely? Is it a role she's playing, like an actress in the movies? Does she have one personality for daytime and another at night? Does she do it to please her bosses and sell more gloves? Or is it simply that the aunt Tititte she knows is not the real one? Or could it be that she is both at once, that every day she passes from one personality to the other as she dodges between two distinct worlds, living at the same time as two mismatched Titittes? Like her mother, who also has two personalities, one for Montcalm Street, the other for the Paradise ... does everyone one day or another end up with two personalities?

She hesitates to go up to the counter, fascinated by this new aunt she didn't even know existed. In any case, maybe she's a woman whose history is quite different from the one she knows as Tititte Desrosiers.

The discussion between the two women continues vigorously. How long will it take Tititte to sell those gloves to this woman who seems so hesitant and can't make up her mind? Will Tititte be able to convince her or will she be obliged to let her go with regret because she is unequal to the confidence Ogilvy's has placed in her? And when the customer leaves, will the other Tititte, the weaker, more sensitive one resurface?

Rhéauna isn't brave enough to interrupt her at work. Anyway, it would all be too complicated: the inevitable worry deep in her aunt's eyes, the incomprehension, the doubt on hearing the unbelievable story she would have to tell to explain why she's here. As well, Rhéauna would be liable to cause Tititte to lose a sale that's already difficult ... She keeps her distance from this lady she doesn't recognize in her role of saleslady in the glove department of a chic store in the west end of Montreal who's supposed to be her mother's sister. Rhéauna edges her way to the exit and ends up on the sidewalk of the grey stone building, disturbed and a little lost. She has to ask someone for directions. Preferably a person who understands her language of course.

Well-dressed pedestrians stroll along the street, often in pairs; gentlemen raise their hats in greeting as if they were on the church steps on Sunday morning. What are they doing on the street at this time of day? Don't they need to work to earn their living? Do they spend their time walking and greeting one another? A horse whinnies as an automobile draws too close. A monster row breaks out between the two drivers. Passersby stop on the sidewalk, a small crowd forms at the curb. People side with one opponent or the other. The driver of the automobile is more arrogant, the one in the calèche is more furious. Some people laugh, others seem to want to join in. Rhéauna goes up to a fairly young gentleman and asks him with all the politeness she can muster for directions to Windsor Street, please. He speaks French with a heavy accent, what he says, though, is very clear: she has walked right past it but it's easy, if she crosses the street she will find Windsor Street three blocks away, because Windsor Street changes its name to Peel at the corner of St. Catherine.

A street that changes its name right in the middle of her walk! She's never seen that before in her life and vows that she will check if he's right when she finds the intersection.

They are gathered around the kitchen table. The air is fragrant with toast, nearly burnt, made on the woodstove Teena lit in the early hours of the morning and the scent of strong coffee passed through a percolator the likes of which Maria has never seen and that apparently had come from England, a gift from Tititte on her return from London. Maria has lifted her feet onto the chair next to hers the way she did as a child in Saskatchewan. She spends her life on her feet and grabs every opportunity to rest her legs. She habitually blows on each sip of whatever she is going to drink even when the coffee is already cold.

"The English drink tea but they sell these great coffee makers ... It looks like it came from Italy. They never seem to use it but they all have one ... in case they need it someday I suppose ..."

All through breakfast Maria, who has shown no sign of pregnancy since wakening, no bloating or retching, glances curiously out the big window that looks out onto a garden devastated by the rain and wind and a wooden shed that used to be the outdoor toilet. "Is that where people go to the toilet? In the middle of the city? In the country I can understand, but ..."

"Didn't you have one in Providence?"

"I never saw one. Don't you think it looks like the ones in our village? I haven't seen one since ... But maybe I didn't see them in Providence, maybe they were hidden better ..."

Here in Montreal her sisters tell her that it is called a *bécosse*, a distortion of *back house*, and they have a good laugh.

"If you say you want to go to the toilet here there are lots of people who won't understand ... You have to say you want the *bécosses* ..."

Maria shakes her head.

"I could never say that! That's way too ugly. *Bécosses!*"

Teena spread a thick layer of maple sugar on a huge slice of bread and butter.

"Do you remember, Mama used to call it a lavatory when we had company and she wanted to speak well?"

Slapped thighs, great bursts of laughter, the memory of summer nights when they had to cut through the flower and vegetable gardens to relieve themselves. The fear of running into creatures of the night, animals or ghosts, the latter more terrifying than the former. And the chamber pots in winter, the chore of emptying them, each one in turn, red with shame and doing all they could to avoid being seen by the others. The jeers sometimes, especially from their father:

"Did you read *La porteuse de pain*, by Xavier de Montépin? Well, what we've got is the carrier of p– …"

His wife, red-faced with anger, always interrupted before he finished his sentence:

"Méo! Watch what you're about to say! You could very well spend tomorrow night in a bakery that doesn't smell one bit like bread!"

Méo would fall silent just in time, wink at his daughters who were laughing, and let through the one who, that morning, had inherited the nasty task.

The aroma of eggs, bacon, maple syrup, all kinds of jam placed in small glass dishes, and of strong cheddar cheese mingled with those of toast and coffee. All three sisters would stay in that cocoon of fragrance and warmth, sheltered from everything and everyone, a nutty trio reunited at last after a separation of so many years and who have too much to tell one another to pay attention to the rest of the world. Two of them haven't shown up at work that morning and will have to pay the consequences; as for the third, she would be very happy to look for work to do during the months she can move comfortably before giving birth. The third pot of coffee is emptied into small cups slowly sipped. Bread crumbs are picked up by a moistened index finger, jam stains wiped up with a damp rag. The conversation languishes after some superficial remarks about breakfast, as if no one can manage to express the essential, that important matter the three sisters should tell one another when they get together over coffee in the morning or if they've decided to play hooky. There are gales of laughter, a few tears are shed, trivial insults tossed off, but the main thing they might have to say to one another remains unspoken and it weighs on them.

True, Teena had delivered her confession the day before and Maria dared not ask any questions about the child brought up in the country, whose existence she'd been unaware of, waiting till she and Teena were alone and Teena was in the mood for confidences again, but what about the discreet Tititte, content as she has always been to follow the conversation of the others without getting too involved? She had listened to Maria's story at Ernest's place, Teena's too, but about her, about her life, her joys, her sorrows – nothing. Still the same mystery surrounded her return from England, never explained, subject to the worst assumptions and the ugliest gossip.

Maria is about to ask her a direct question when Tititte coughs into her fist, a sign that she is going to say something.

"I have to go back to Ogilvy's at noon, girls ... I told them I was going to the doctor. A doctor's appointment doesn't take the whole day, they're liable to ask questions."

Teena got up to wash the coffee maker in the sink.

"I have to be home at noon too. Somebody has to sell those damn shoes at L.N. Messier, I'm the only saleslady with a brain in her head ... Monsieur Desbaillets, who works with me, most of the time just gawks at women's legs ... the ones who agree to be served by a man and aren't the most respectable if you get what I mean ... Stay here, Maria, as you can see there's tons of room ... Settle down, unpack your suitcase, go for a walk in the neighbourhood ...

"I don't want to bother you ..."

"You aren't bothering me. You're my sister and I haven't seen you in twelve years. It's a lot better than renting a dirty, depressing room on Mont-Royal Avenue. That you probably couldn't afford anyway."

"I'm going to look for a job first thing tomorrow morning, I promise."

"You don't have to throw yourself into job-hunting on your first morning here ... You wouldn't know where to go ... I'll ask at Messier's ..."

Her coffee finished, Tititte in turn gets up and takes her cup to the sink, places it on top of the dirty dishes.

"I can ask at Ogilvy's too, in case they need someone ... Maybe it wouldn't be in sales at the beginning and Ogilvy's is a long way from here, but we'll see."

"If it's to work as a cleaning lady, forget it ... The last thing I want is to scrub floors in a department store between midnight and four in the morning! I may be poor, with nothing to look forward to, but I've got my pride!"

"You think cleaning ladies don't have pride?"

"That's not what I said."

"It's exactly what you said, Maria. And if that's what they offer, then take it for now, it's better than nothing."

"In my condition?"

"Some women in your condition have done a lot worse."

"I was working in a cotton mill in Providence, Tititte, I know about that! I'm not coming home from vacation! And I'd probably have stayed hitched to my machine till I gave birth if I'd stayed there."

"You can think about that some other day."

They wash the dishes as they'd done when they were little girls and fought to avoid washing them, give themselves a quick sponge bath, get dressed – Tititte, claiming that she's never gone to work in the same dress two days in a row, is afraid someone will notice – and Teena convinces Maria to walk to work with her to get to know the neighbourhood. They are about to leave the apartment on Fullum Street apartment when Tititte takes off her hat and sits down in one of the living-room chairs. The other two look at each other, frowning. Teena goes up to her:

"Tititte! We're leaving!"

Tititte looks her straight in the eyes.

"I've got something to tell you."

146

Teena and Maria have the same idea and conceal their hilarity behind their hands.

"I know what you're thinking … but one pregnant Desrosiers is enough for now. In my case it would be degrading, like for Teena, there'd have been nothing to laugh at. And this is no time for jokes. Come and sit down."

Maria and Teena sit side-by-side on the big sofa, take off their hats and gloves and unbutton their coats.

"For ages now you've been wanting to know what happened in London …"

Teena claps her hands like a four-year-old. Tititte sighs, exasperated.

"Teena! I just said this is no time for jokes!"

"It's not a joke! I'm happy for real!"

"That's fine, but you're thirty-seven years old! A self-respecting woman of thirty-seven doesn't clap her hands like that."

"My Lord! Where did you come up with that one? Just because I'm thirty-seven it doesn't mean I can't show that I'm happy!"

"Just hold back a little, Teena, that's all I ask. What I've decided to say to you is hard to confess and it takes all my guts. You two told your stories yesterday and I just sat by the window like a turkey, like someone who's never lived. I was always shy and I was always a listener but I want to talk too, you know!"

"We didn't know that, Tititte. You always refused to talk before! For years!"

Tititte lowers her head.

"These things aren't easy to admit … and … you can't say that Ernest understands women's things."

"If you ask me, Ernest doesn't understand much …"

They smile in spite of themselves, the good old complicity of the Desrosiers sisters settles into the living room, curled up in their midst like a sleeping cat.

"Take your coats off … I might be a while."

After calm is restored – it is as if a fourth person is present in the room, so much have the coats, hats, and gloves on the second armchair taken on a human form – Tititte closes her eyes for a few seconds before launching into her story.

"Me, it wasn't a good physique that's responsible for what happened to me. Teena saw him, she'll tell you ..."

Teena opens her eyes wide and slaps the arm of her easy chair.

"I said, it's no time for jokes! And he wasn't so ugly you'd make a face, Teena! If you don't want me to say anything I can stop right now, you know ..."

Teena raises one hand as a sign of peace, apologizes.

"Go on, I won't say anything."

Tititte settles comfortably in her chair, arranges her dress around her, clears her throat.

"I was an old maid too, time was passing ... but it didn't bother me. I had a good job at Morgan's – Ogilvy's hadn't been built yet back then – Teena and I were the only women who earned their own living, who were independent ... We were proud of that ... But then I met a man so different from the ones I'd known till then that ... yes, I was taken in. You can't say I fell head-over-heels in love like Teena, no, it wasn't that ... it was more ... I don't know ... He knew things that others didn't, he never talked about things that didn't interest me, he wasn't nice just to ... you know what I mean ... He didn't want just *that* and it showed. He was English from England and he was here for a few months, then he'd go home because his job was finished. He worked for a famous department store in London – Harrods – and he'd come here to see if Harrods could buy Morgan's or something like that, I don't remember ... And don't worry, he wasn't ... he wasn't what Papa used to call a confirmed bachelor with girlish manners, if you know what I mean, I'd've realized it and kept my distance ... But his gallantry, his manners, his grooming, his sense of humour all made me get over my hesitation. Because I used to be ... I was hesitant! I thought, he's a funny one, that guy, is it because he's ugly that he doesn't make the first move? He wasn't so ugly he was scary, no, but in a group of men he'd have been pretty well the last one I'd choose ... Though I went out with ... And I always enjoyed myself ... Always the right word, always the right choice of movies … All that to tell you that one thing led to another till one evening he asked me to follow him to London. A proper marriage proposal, kneeling to ask me, the works … It was the first time a man had knelt in front me and, I'm telling you, it did the trick! It was probably a sudden urge that made me say yes, I knew it was idiotic, it was happening too fast, it was a decision that had to be mulled over … But … I don't know … maybe the prospect of leaving a life that was already mapped out with no chance of change, of taking the boat to England and living in London, one of the biggest cities in the world … It's true that it wasn't for him that I said yes, it wasn't because I wanted to marry him, that it may have been just the Desrosiers disease that had infected me, the move, the adventure, the unknown over there, far away, where everything might be better … He was one of the rare Englishmen who was Catholic, I wouldn't even have to change religion … I don't know … I don't know … I didn't even hesitate before I boarded the ship, didn't ask myself any questions, despite everything Teena and Ernest had told me, I just … I just … It was like diving into a mystery, do you see what I mean? To take advantage of an opportunity that would never, ever come again, to take a chance, that's it, to take a chance, to risk everything, elsewhere, far away. The Journey. All the Desrosiers have travelled thinking happiness is waiting for them elsewhere and they all end up wanting to set off on an adventure again … That's how we're made … Crazy, isn't it? My passion wasn't for the man who was taking me to London but for the life he promised me. That was a bad reason to get married, I knew that, but I said yes all the same. And lived to regret it."

She takes a handkerchief from her purse.

"It isn't because I want to cry that I'm taking this out, it's because it's hot …"

Teena smiles a sad little smile.

"It's cooler already, Tititte. I let the coal furnace go out because we were going out. You're too young for hot flashes, aren't you?"

Tititte fans herself with her hanky, cheeks red, forehead sweating.

"I'm the oldest, it makes sense for me to be the first."

The other two look at each other. So they were at that stage. Their older sister had already started her menopause … Maria places her hands on her belly. The last-chance baby … How she was going to love him despite the problems he would lead to.

Tititte still held the handkerchief …

"He didn't want to get married here – you understand, I just had a brother and a sister in Montreal while he had all kinds of relatives waiting for him in London – so he took two cabins on the ship. A dream. The train trip to New York, crossing the Atlantic, five days reading on chaises longues, eating, and playing badminton – that's right, there was a badminton court on the ship, even a theatre where they showed movies – the arrival in Southampton, all that … Then London! I thought it was so beautiful at the beginning, if you only knew … It was the beginning of autumn, and the parks – there are so many you can't count them – were magnificent. In any case, before the damn rain started … Everyone in his family seemed happy that James was marrying, you understand, he was past thirty-five. We didn't have a honeymoon because we'd come from the other end of the world … You must suspect that it all was hiding something … Everything was too perfect … as if there hadn't been enough problems! That he didn't make advances on the ship I could understand, I was Catholic too and I wouldn't have let him, promise of marriage or not … Excuse me, Teena, but I get the impression I'm more prudish than you …"

Astonished that her sister would criticize her in the middle of her confession, Teena startles then shrugs her shoulders.

"When you're in love you aren't, Tititte! There's no Catholic religion that lasts … You must not have been in love, that's all …"

"You're right, I guess I was flattered more than anything else … in love with the journey …"

The other two think she is going to cry this time or at least that she is going to wipe the sweat that streaks her cheeks; no, all she does is play with the little square of cotton, fiddle with it without bringing it to her face.

"I don't know what I was expecting actually, I thought I'd been pretty stupid for not having more experience, for *really* not knowing what to do with a man, but anyway on the wedding night he wasn't any more enterprising … He wished me good night after he'd kissed my forehead and murmured a not very convincing *I love you.* Let me tell you, that was a surprise! I put it down to shyness, reserve, fatigue … I don't know … respect … But days and weeks went by and he still stayed on his side of the bed without seeming to want to cross it … Of course all kinds of things went through my mind … First of all, to find out why he'd wanted to marry me if he didn't want to do it with me … For a minute I even thought he really was a confirmed bachelor and that he'd just married me to hide … But he didn't go out at night, he wasn't effeminate, and he was so nice with me I suppose I chose to believe him …"

This time it is a genuine hot flash. Her face turns bright red, she undoes the top buttons of her dress, fans herself with her handkerchief.

"The most embarrassing thing is when it happens at the store … I can hardly manage to hide it. Anyway, getting back to my story … The days were definitely getting shorter, I had nothing to do but wait for him, to fix his supper … and then … You know we talk about the rain in England, the beautiful gardens and the women's complexions that are luminous because it rains all the time, but … you have no idea. London is a big city, millions and millions of people live there, everybody heats with coal, which makes a kind of yellow fog that sticks in your throat, that chokes you, you try to get your breath, you run after it … It can rain for weeks at a time without ever showing a single little spot of blue sky, it falls like nails, it's damp, even gas stoves can't kill the humidity. It pierces you to the bone … The English don't understand that we're cold because we come from Canada where it's dry and they laugh in our faces when we tell them we've never been as cold as we are in London. I wore a sweater all day long, sometimes I even wore my winter coat in the house I was so frozen!"

She stops to look at her two sisters.

"I know I'm beating around the bush, saying whatever comes to mind so I won't get to the important things … No, that's not true, I think it's important to know what kind of state I was in … Understand, I'd crossed a large part of the world to get married, then months later I wasn't married yet! Before the Church, sure, but not factually. I'd even reached the point of not wondering when he'd make up his mind, as if I'd known that he never would! And then the damn rain! The damn fog! The damn fog! It's all everybody talks about, the fog, the damn fog, everything's always the fault of the fog! Four times I got lost on my own street because of the damn fog!"

She gets up, charges across the room, and flings open the window.

"Sorry. I have to breathe."

She presses her forehead against the cold glass, takes several deep breaths, wiping her face with her handkerchief.

"Can you tell me why not one of the three of us has managed to find a husband that makes any sense? Can you? All the women our age have been married a long time, they have children to raise while the rest of us … You two have children, true, but you're all alone anyway and I couldn't say that you look really happy! Teena's never had a husband, Maria had one but from what she says he was no prize, there's nothing good to be said about him, and then there's me …"

She comes back, sits down …

"I still say whatever comes into my head … But we haven't been lucky, it's true!"

She blows her nose, dabs her eyes.

"Listen … What do we do nowadays. Eh? What do we do? I got married but at the same time I wasn't married. It was more like I was a ladies' companion, but instead of taking care of an old woman, I was taking care of a young man. I saw myself putting up with that for years, walled up inside my beautiful London flat, saying nothing and moping around, getting older married but still an old maid. Anyway, I finally decided to talk to him, to confront him, ask for explanations …"

She gets up and starts to pace the living room, a hard thing to do given the small size of the room. She goes from the sofa to the door, from the door to the window she's left partly open despite the cold, then comes back to her armchair where she doesn't sit down.

"Have the rest of you ever heard of that – a man who's frigid? I'd never have thought it could exist! That's not what he told me of course, he didn't use that word, he handled it with white gloves, he got lost in all sorts of complicated explanations, he tried to attract my sympathy, my pity, but that's still what he meant. I had to end up with the only man in the world who didn't like doing it! I didn't deserve that! He told me he'd always been that way, that he was attracted to women, he thought they were beautiful, exciting, but he didn't like … He liked what came before, the courting, the excitement, the heart pounding – all of that, but nothing of what goes on during. Have you two ever heard such a thing? And a European on top of it! Frigid women, sure, I know tons of them, most of the women I know don't like it and they put up with it because it's their duty. But a man! According to them, men never get enough! You can't imagine … The humiliation … I felt …"

She plunks herself down in her chair. A tree falling down. She leans her head on the back of the chair and shuts her eyes.

"I felt like the last of the last of the worst, that's how I felt. The most unattractive woman in the world. I knew that I wasn't desired by my own husband, that he would always treat me as a trinket, a decorative doll that you sit on the coverlet after you've made the bed, that it was true, finally, that I'd go on fretting in my hole, far from everyone I knew, with no hope of ever … I wasn't about to take a lover like they do in French novels, I'm no slut! I was practically thirty years old and my life was over! Maybe that's why he'd chosen me. Because I'd come from far away and couldn't defend myself. He had no choice but to marry to save appearances, so he'd chosen a poor Canadian woman with no resources. Well, let me tell you, he saw that I had resources, I had plenty! You can't imagine everything I had to say to him. The insults I was able to let fly, all the names I called him! Even *faggot*, though I knew that wasn't true. At least not if I believed what he'd just told me. He asked me on bended knee to forgive him, he bawled like a girl, he was in such a pitiful state that I felt like spanking him! I actually wondered if I'd done that and then chose to forget it afterwards … I was humiliated and I humiliated him, I'm telling you, we were a handsome couple! So then, right away, before it was too late and I changed my mind – that's what he was trying to do, damn him, to have me through pity – I told him I was asking for our marriage to be annulled … He begged me not to do that, that it would destroy his reputation, that he'd be forced to go into exile as far away as Australia or South Africa to hide his shame, so I decided to load it all onto my back, to take all the blame, to say that everything was my fault, that we could claim that I missed my family too much, that I was sick, that I was the frigid one, anything, anything to get myself out of there, to leave London, leave behind the fog, board the ship again, come home and take refuge here, forget everything else or at least try to! But … an annulment would've been public, it would end up being known, he could have lost everything, what he called his male pride in any case … Imagine … A man like that talking about pride! A man who likes to spoil his wife in every respect but the right one!"

She gets up, furious. Her rage makes the veins in her neck swell, crossing her arms and folding in half as if she's had a cramp.

"So it means I'm still married!"

She goes back to the window.

"To that *thing*! Not even because he was Catholic like me but to save his reputation! I'm his sick wife who couldn't stand the London climate, who had to go back to the pure air of her far-off Canada, then he became the poor innocent, victim of a woman too weak to brave the goddamn fog! You should've see the look on his parents' faces when we told them we had no choice but to separate! I felt as if I were living in a melodrama at the Théâtre National! Sometimes I think what goes on in those plays is ridiculous but what I was living through was even worse!"

She turns around, sits on the windowsill. She starts a gesture that she doesn't finish.

"It feels good, a little cool air on your back. Even though I'm liable to wake up tomorrow with a backache ..."

Teena and Maria hesitate to intervene. Actually they don't know how to react, if their sister expects words of consolation or wants reassurance from them, or if she prefers to finish her confession uninterrupted. They'd have taken her in their arms, rocked her like a child with a nightmare, they would have told her to forget all that, that nothing was keeping her from making a new life for herself, the world was full of men who would ask for nothing better than to have a wife like her at their side, that she was still young, pretty, attractive. They are on the point of saying so, of crossing the living room, of going to her, of taking her away from the window where the cold wind rushes in and is liable to make her sick ... They stand frozen there, frozen in the face of Tititte's helplessness, preferring respectful silence to words that are going to sound tactless. And pointless.

It is Tititte herself, finally, who breaks the silence.

"Any word about this to our brother, Ernest, and I'll strangle you one by one."

They laugh. Because a reaction is necessary to start the motor of life again, put an end to this essential but unfortunate digression that is bringing them closer together without providing the words of consolation all three need. Without even consulting one another, they all go to the kitchen, where Teena makes one last coffee. Ogilvy's and L.N. Messier can wait a little longer, the Desrosiers sisters need to be together in silent communion before they throw themselves headlong into their complicated existences.

And it is arm in arm that they leave the apartment on Fullum Street.

They go along Mont-Royal to the L.N. Messier store between Fabre and Garnier, where Teena leaves her two sisters to go inside and sell shoes. Tititte and Maria window-shop for a while where they are advertising Venetian sheets for forty-three cents and Bruges lace for four cents a yard. Then Tititte turns to Maria.

"D'you feel like walking? Ogilvy's is at the other end of the city but it would help you get to know Montreal."

"How long would it take?"

"A good couple of hours ... Unless you're afraid to walk in your condition ..."

"No, it's not that ... I had a good rest last night ... But how would I get back?"

"Like you did yesterday, you'll take the streetcar."

"Which way should we walk?"

"Along Mont-Royal to St. Lawrence, St. Lawrence to St. Catherine, then we'll turn right and go as far as Ogilvy's ..."

"Are we dressed warmly enough?"

"We'll walk quickly, that warms you up."

They have rediscovered the Desrosiers sisters' way of starting an endless and pointless conversation, questions and answers exchanged at top speed, more to fill the silence than to express anything important, reassuring prattle that won't end until they've come to the end of their stroll, glad to be together and already forgetting the difficult confessions expressed in pain.

He leans on the marble counter and laughs. A long laugh.

Puzzled and nonplussed, Rhéauna looks at him frowning.

"Why're you laughing like that?"

He straightens up, wipes his eyes.

"I'm sorry ... But did you really think you'd be able to take three people to Saskatchewan with seven dollars and eleven cents?"

Yet she'd chosen her ticket seller carefully. Entering Windsor Station she headed immediately towards the wickets, a long row of counters in marble and wrought iron that looked more like bank tellers' booths – her mother has a small savings account at the Caisse Desjardins, of which she is very proud, and she visits the St. Catherine Street branch as often as she can, even with Rhéauna for whom these obligatory stops are deadly boring – the wickets looked more like a bank than a place where you could buy train tickets. She studied each ticket seller, looking for the friendliest. She listened to them talk with travellers, she checked which one spoke French, she decided that the one for her was a big jovial man who seemed to take the time to advise his clients rather than serve them in a hurry and without a word like most of the others. She took her place at the end of his line, which was rather short – thank the Lord – craning her neck and checking the time. She would be late but not too late ... An old lady in front of her is taking ages to pay for her ticket: open the purse, take out the wallet, rummage in the wallet, close the wallet, shut the purse, pay for the ticket, open the purse again, take out the wallet, open the wallet, stow her change, close the wallet, put it back in the purse, close the purse, put the wallet back in the purse, put the ticket in the purse, close the purse – and Rhéauna shows her impatience by tapping her foot and sighing. Then, after several long minutes, she finds herself facing the ticket seller, who frowns at the sight of her.

"On your own?"

"Yes. My mother sent me."

First lie. Feeling herself go red, she coughs into her fist.

"What can I do for you, sweetheart."

As she is saying it, just when the words are about to leave her mouth, when she is about to ask for three tickets to Saskatoon, Saskatchewan, if you please, sir, they're for my mother and my little brother and me – she had prepared the sentence when she set out from the Montcalm Street apartment – she has a brief dizzy spell. She feels the blood rise to her head, a certain weakness in her legs, her heart begins to beat too quickly, and all the absurdity of her project strikes her at once. She's done it all for nothing. She knows that. She's always known. She has done it to let herself believe that the reunion with her two sisters is still possible, to keep herself from falling into hopelessness; she has used as a pretext the dangers of war – and later her mother's difficult life – to pursue an impossible, ridiculous dream. She has made definite moves – breaking her piggy bank, lying to her mother, crossing the city on foot – to come this far, to this station, to the brink of leaving. She'd had a few sparks of consciousness while she was walking, like outside the Paradise, but every time she had chased them away, preferring to deny the evidence and take shelter in the illusion of a return to her former life. All that because she wants her Saskatchewan life to be returned to her. Her fortune.

She still recites her story but with less conviction than she would have liked.

And he laughs.

"Poor you, you couldn't even buy a child's ticket with that much money. The train is expensive, you know!"

He leans over to her again, rests his elbows on the marble counter, assumes a fatherly air.

"And even if you'd had enough money, even if you'd taken out a big fat hundred-dollar bill, do you think I'd have sold you three tickets for Saskatchewan? Do you think I'd have given three tickets to Saskatchewan to a little girl like you? Even if you say your mother sent you? I wouldn't have had the right! Come on, we only sell tickets to adults." An idea seems to cross his mind and he straightens up.

"Listen here, you, did you sneak away from home? Are you a runaway? Tell me? Did you run away from your mother's place after stealing seven dollars and eleven cents so you could take the train somewhere, anywhere, even Saskatchewan?"

Again she's being seen as a thief!

Rhéauna is convinced that he is going to sound the alarm, call the police who'll arrest her, take her home by the scruff of her neck, denounce her to her mother, punish her, even put her in jail. She has to pee right away, as she had at Dupuis Frères. She has to pee, right there, right now, or there could be an accident!

The ticket seller is glaring at her now. She has to leave, she has to find the bathroom, she has to pee before it's too late. She runs, she can barely hear him ask again if she's a runaway, if her mother knows she's here, if she has stolen the money ... As she passes the big clock she realizes that it's a quarter to noon. Even if she takes the streetcar she's going to be very late. Meanwhile, there's something more urgent ... Yes, *Toilettes – Restrooms*, she has been saved for the time being. She rushes into the bathroom, jostling an old lady who walks with a cane, and takes refuge in a stall which is also lined with marble. Just in time, thank God, just in time.

It's taken her three hours to come this far, she's got through *Little Red Riding Hood* and *Alice in Wonderland*, she has struck down an electric dragon and experienced a great love, she has met all kinds of people and lived unbelievable adventures and everything has been sorted out in three minutes! She didn't even have time to react when her dream shattered into a thousand pieces. She sits there for quite a while, underpants around her ankles.

If only she could cry.

She is sitting on a wooden bench in a park across from a huge hotel that reminds her a little of the Château Laurier in Ottawa, home of her great cousin Ti-Lou, with its high corner tower, its ogival windows, its air of a false fortress. It is called the Hotel Windsor.

On her way out of the station going north up Windsor Street, Rhéauna noticed that it was past noon and instead of hopping onto the first streetcar that would appear on St. Catherine Street, she has come here to take refuge, on the edge of the beautiful park in the sweltering heat of this early afternoon that can't decide whether to let its storms burst. The air is oppressive, hard to breathe, the clouds are lower and darker than ever, you can sense the imminent arrival of a tremendous rainfall, downpours that may perhaps rinse and cool this too-heavy August day. It's been threatening for too long, it's hard on the nerves, it has to burst once and for all!

She sits with her elbows on her knees, head resting on her hands to think. What can she tell her mother to explain why she's late? Another lie? Make up a story to explain why she went out to buy school supplies and came back three hours later empty-handed? Keep it all to herself? Or be content with confiding in a hushed voice to Théo, unburden her heart in front of him, because she knows that he won't understand a word of what she tells him?

Or run even farther away, heading west along St. Catherine until fatigue makes it impossible for her to carry on, until someone wonders what this little girl in a red dress is doing there, wandering aimlessly so late at night, in the middle of the night, at dawn, until the police arrest her and take her home, shoving her at her mother who is worried to death?

A genuine runaway?

No, that's not like her. She will have to confront reality, the consequences of her ridiculous adventure, though without confessing everything to her mother, who would be liable to lose confidence in her.

She is about to get up and head for St. Catherine Street, a weight in place of her heart, when the old woman who took an eternity to pay for her train ticket comes and sits on the bench beside her.

"You look like you've lost half of everything you own."

"I think I've lost everything and more."

The woman smiles, obviously relieved by her answer.

"Are you lost? Do you even know what part of town you're in?"

She speaks in a strange way, in an accent Rhéauna has never heard, which is neither that of Montrealers nor that of the French from France but a mixture of the two, as if she were trying to sound like a European while still rolling her *R*s like the inhabitants of Montreal.

"Yes, I know where I am and, no, I'm not lost."

"I have a good two hours till the train leaves so I decided to walk around the station … and then I spotted you in your pretty red dress when you came out of the ladies' room. You were trying to buy a train ticket, weren't you?"

This time Rhéauna gets to her feet, ready to leave.

"I haven't run away if that's what you think."

"I didn't say I thought you'd run away but I confess that I found it rather odd for a little girl like you to be buying a train ticket …"

"… so you followed me!"

"No, I didn't follow you. But as I continued my walk I found you here, prostrate on your bench, and I wondered what you were doing … It's not every day that you find a little girl sitting all alone on a park bench. May I ask, do you … do you have a problem?"

Something about this woman is reassuring. She doesn't feel she is being judged. That's it, this lady asks questions without having decided in advance what answers she expects. Without judging her. And such goodness emanates from her grey eyes sparkling with mischief that in a matter of minutes Rhéauna has told her everything, it all comes out in perfect order, clearly, chronologically, and expressed properly: Saskatchewan, her return to Montreal last year, her little brother, Théo, of whose very existence she'd been unaware of, her mother whom she was with again after so many years but so different from her memories of her, the danger of war that was lying in wait for them all and that she wanted to spare them – her mother, her little brother, and herself. She can hear herself talking, she listens to herself telling a perfect stranger what she would never dare confide to her own mother; she can't help it, it just comes out, with strange ease, and as her improvised confession pours out she feels a tremendous sense of relief, as if it were raining on her, as if the clouds had finally burst and the water from the sky were washing her and making her lighter. She doesn't feel like crying as people do when they confess a grave sin; on the contrary, if she hadn't held herself back she would have jumped up and down, clapping her hands. How strange it is! Yes, it's strange to feel so many things at the same time while she listens to herself tell with such happiness secrets one might have thought inexpressible.

As soon as she's finished, however, her anxiety returns. She sits back down on the wooden bench.

"I don't know what to tell my mother … I'm scared I'll disappoint her and I'm scared of being punished. I know I deserve a punishment, a big one too, but … you understand, she trusts me so much … What should I do?"

She knows in advance what the old lady will tell her because it's the only thing to do.

"Tell her everything. Don't be afraid. If she's a sensible woman, she'll understand. Is she a sensible woman?"

Rhéauna nods her head.

"Here's what you should do … It's too late to take the streetcar, you're right about that, so you're going to take a taxi."

"I've never taken a taxi by myself …"

"Have you ever travelled in a streetcar by yourself?"

"Yes."

"It's no more complicated, you'll see … Look, across the street there are three taxis waiting in front of the Hotel Windsor … I'll talk to the driver, he'll take good care of you. Where do you live?"

"On Montcalm Street."

The lady frowns.

"You don't know where it is, do you?"

The lady looks down, embarrassed.

"No, not really … I know it's in the east end …"

"It's way far east. It took me quite a while to walk this far … You don't live in the east end, do you?"

"Look, we're not here to talk about me but you're right, I don't live in the east end … Do you have any money? Oh yes, how stupid I am, you have the money for the train tickets …"

"That's my own money, I told you …"

"So you're going to sacrifice part of it to take a taxi … You're going to go home, you're going to tell your mother everything, you may not even have to ask her to forgive you because you did it with the best intentions in the world …"

"You don't know my mother … Not only will I have to ask her to forgive me, I'll probably be punished for a long time …"

"No mother would punish her child after such a beautiful proof of love … What you did is so beautiful you won't be punished for it …"

Rhéauna listens to her, fascinated. She feels as if she is in a novel by the Comtesse de Ségur. The chic lady is speaking to her in a language she has only found in books, as if a kind fairy godmother had emerged from the pages of *Les malheurs de Sophie* or an old fairy from a fantasy tale is helping to bring to a logical conclusion a madcap adventure that was liable to end abruptly. And imagine, earlier she'd thought this old lady was ridiculous because she'd taken so long to pay for her train ticket. What would she have done if this good fairy hadn't intervened, where would she have gone, where would she have ended up? She realizes she'll never know as she finds herself letting the old woman lead her by the hand to the taxis.

After she's asked Rhéauna where exactly Montcalm Street is, the old lady speaks to the driver in English. The only thing Rhéauna understands is that the lady is telling the driver to take Dorchester Street, no doubt because there's less traffic on it and it will be faster ...

She leans over the door to the back seat of the cab.

"Are you going to do everything I told you?"

Rhéauna's not sure but she nods her head. After all, she has to please this unhoped-for good Samaritan, reassure her, make her believe that everything will go as she hopes, she deserves that. "Good luck. And ... stop thinking about the war. The war will not come here. It's their problem over there ... You're in no danger. Neither is your family."

The old lady who's stepped out of a book waves to her with a gloved hand as the taxi, backfiring, drives away from the Hotel Windsor. Rhéauna wonders if it was her aunt Tititte who'd sold her the gloves. And if she had taken ages to pay for them. Open the handbag, rummage in it, take out the change purse ... She can't help smiling despite her anxiety and thinks to herself that she will remember this woman for the rest of her life. Then she realizes that she hasn't even thanked her. She turns around. The good fairy is in the same place, hand raised, very frail all of a sudden, you might think she's smaller, as if she were going to vanish into the air, evaporate and return to the pages of the storybook from which she'd escaped.

Rhéauna sighs.

"Thank you, Madame."

Just as the taxi is turning left onto Dorchester, the sky is ripped apart in a tremendous peal of thunder and begins to pour down on Montreal, which needs it badly, torrents of tepid water that will drench everything in a few seconds. It's through a curtain of rain – happy that the taxi is a closed vehicle – that Rhéauna crosses the city – this time by car.

When she steps inside the apartment on Montcalm Street after divesting herself of a whole dollar made up of five, ten, and twenty-five cent pieces, no tip because she doesn't know that such a thing exists, she finds her mother sitting at the kitchen table over two plates of macaroni that have no doubt been waiting there for a good long while and have had time to cool off. Théo must be having his nap because she doesn't hear him gurgling in that language only he understands.

Her mother's frown, the dark look she shoots at her as she approaches the table and settles over her plate of macaroni, tells her all she needs to know about the stage of concern and confusion she's in.

"I found your piggy bank in pieces in the garbage. I think you've got some explaining to do."

SECOND PRELUDE BY WAY OF A CODA

MONTREAL

Montreal is an enormous city, taking longer to cross than Saskatoon or Winnipeg, and Rhéauna keeps her nose plastered to the window of the car that at a brisk pace is taking them – her mother, her brother, and her – through streets jam-packed with vehicles of all kinds. She dares not look in her mother's direction, not yet. And Maria remains silent in the face of her daughter's obstinate manner. Climbing into the taxi, she has simply murmured: "We'll talk back at the house." Now and then the baby wails and Rhéauna feels her heart sink. She would have been glad to be home if it weren't for this surprise. She had come to join her mother, not a new family! A baby changes everything, it's the centre of attraction, it wears you out, it weighs you down, you have to take care of it all the time; she remembers Alice was a year and a half old when the three Rathier sisters crossed the continent for the first time and Rhéauna had to take care of everything during the train trip. But at the end of it, there'd been her grandmother who had taken over everything as soon as they arrived while here ... It is obvious that her mother isn't interested in her, that she's had Rhéauna come here just to look after her little brother, that it isn't her mother's love for her that had made her act but the need ... the need for a servant, yes, that's it, the need to have within reach a servant who wouldn't cost anything but would be obliged to obey her.

She glances surreptitiously in her mother's direction and at the bundle wrapped in a blue blanket from which emerges now and then some jerky sounds that aren't even words. Yet that profile ... She had dreamed so much about her mother's beautiful profile ... The biggish nose – like her own actually – the high cheekbones, the intelligent brow, the eyes that sometimes spoke more eloquently than the mouth, all the hair you could imagine under a big hat, her skin that smelled so good when she got out of her bath, shouting to her girls to jump in because the water was still clean and fairly warm. The laughter that overcame her though she hadn't seen it coming, even her sudden and nearly incomprehensible rages because she couldn't take any more: the still-absent husband, the lack of work, three children to feed ... All that followed, with no warning, by periods of giggles and tickles in a house wrecked by games invented on the spot, made up in order to forget, or forgive, scenes of despondency that were too long and too brutal. And no doubt traumatizing for the children who knew nothing about life. The endless bedtime stories, inspired by something called *The Arabian Nights* that Rhéauna wasn't familiar with yet. She had heard of Ali Baba for the first time, and of Aladdin, she had felt the desert wind, dreamed about the desert roses that grew without water, and followed the stories of Scheherazade whom she called *Chère Rasade*, because she didn't understand her name ... And goodness. The goodness of her mother who always found a way to go on in spite of everything, to land on her feet ... That was what she wanted to find again, just that, not an extra baby who is going to complicate their lives. Take care of her little sisters, yes, any time, no matter when, she is used to that, she adores them and is ready to do anything to keep them close to her all her life if she has to, but this ... this ... bundle of problems filled with poop that have to be changed dozens of time every day, she doesn't want that, especially if it's the only reason for her to be in Montreal!

The apartment, on a street where all the houses are three-storeys high, is large and quite pleasant; Rhéauna is disappointed, though, to see that she has to share a room with her new little brother. In Maria, she and her two sisters slept in the same room, true, and it wasn't always easy, but she knew them, she'd spent her life with them, whereas she knows nothing at all about this bundle of rags of whom all she's seen is the face, in the taxi, and almost surreptitiously because Maria didn't want him to catch cold because of the air rushing into the car despite the heat.

As soon as Rhéauna has checked out the whole apartment – the two bedrooms, living room, huge kitchen, bathroom – Maria dumps Théo in his bed and undresses him the way you unwrap a candy, with tremendous care and a greedy look on her face. He squirms and gurgles, Rhéauna can see him through the bars of his bassinet. She has decided not to let herself be touched by this pretty picture and is nearly sulking, sitting on what is going to be her bed, arms crossed over her chest.

His diaper changed, his little bum powdered, Maria finally turns to her daughter.

"C'mere, I've got something important to tell you ..."

Rhéauna approaches her somewhat reluctantly, thinking her mother is going to sing the praises of Théo. But Maria kneels beside the bed, puts her arms around her daughter's waist, and talks to her very gently, holding her tight.

"I'm going to tell you things as they are. First of all, you could never imagine how much I've missed you. A mother separated from her children is a dead woman, Nana. What I did, you know was because I couldn't do otherwise, Nana, I hope you know that and you believe me ... It was for your own good, so that you would have a normal childhood, because I wouldn't have been able to give you that ... But you know that and you've always understood because you're a smart girl."

Maria hesitates a few seconds before continuing. She has rested her head on Rhéauna's shoulder and now the girl smells the perfume of her mother's hair for the first time in five years and she nearly bursts into sobs. Oh Lord! She had forgotten it! Not the others, not the perfume Maria wore to go out on Saturday night and that clung to her clothes, or the prickly smell of sweat during the heat wave that fell over Providence every year but this one, yes, of freshly washed hair, the piquant scent of the shampoo with the good smell of soap, it suddenly comes back to her, it makes her want to throw her arms around her mother and cry for hours.

"I also have to tell you that I started a job a while ago, working nights. I work from seven in the evening till after midnight, so I had to find someone to look after Théo. And that's expensive."

Rhéauna stiffens in her arms; Maria tightens her embrace.

"You have to listen all the way to the end, Nana … It's true, I feel like you've guessed, that I brought you here to take care of your little brother … But don't think it's just for that, that I didn't miss you, that I didn't want to see you and your sisters. It's just … it's just that I found a way to make you come back … You, first of all, to help me … To help me with Théo and get things ready for when your two sisters come … When I've finished talking, Nana, you're going to tell me what they're like, what kind of little girls they are, whether Béa eats as much as she used to, whether *you* eat as much too … I want to know everything about you girls but … Look, school starts next week and I've enrolled you in a very nice convent called the Académie Garneau that's run by nuns who are strict but who'll give you a good education … You'll learn all kinds of things you'd never have learned in Saskatchewan, you'll become a clever little girl, you'll see, and when your sisters arrive they won't recognize you … And at night, when I go to work, you're going to look after him. You're old enough, Grandma told me you're very serious, very responsible … You'll see, he's the furthest thing from a brat. He sleeps after his bottle, he's always smiling, he's quiet, and if he ever doesn't sleep through the night I'll take care of him, you'll stay in bed because you'll have to go to school … And next year, next summer, when school's out … we'll bring your little sisters here. Would you like that? They'll make the same journey you did. They'll come and join you in Montreal. And we'll be happy, all of us together, you'll see … We'll move to a bigger house, Alice and Béa will go to the same school as you, you'll go on taking care of Théo … Tell me you understand, tell me you're glad to be here, tell me you'll be happy here with me and Théo, I need to hear you say that, Nana, I need to know that you won't be unhappy very long, because I know you're unhappy, I can see it on your face and I understand, I've cut you off from everything you know, I'm asking you to make a tremendous sacrifice, but tell me you won't be mad at me for very long. I had no choice, Nana, I had no choice."

Rhéauna turns around and looks her straight in the eye. And what passes between them is simply their failure to understand.

ABOUT THE SERIES

Crossing the City is the second in Michel Tremblay's Desrosiers Diaspora series. These historical novels reconstruct the childhood and adolescence of Rhéauna, or Nana, who is beloved to readers of Quebec literature as The Fat Woman Next Door. Based on Tremblay's mother, Nana is, as an adult, a central character in the Chronicles of the Plateau Mont-Royal.

As the series opens, Rhéauna must leave the shelter of her grandparents' Saskatchewan farmhouse to live with her mother in bustling Montreal. Along the way, Rhéauna meets and begins to understand her many mysterious aunts, including her mother's once-estranged sisters. These unmarried women become significant presences in Nana's adolescent life, even as her own faraway sisters and grandparents stay close to her young heart. Her longing for home is eclipsed, as the series progresses, only by her longing to understand her strange and changing society; in each novel Nana is faced with some new form of duplicity in the adult world, and her responses will come to define her own entrance into that world.

The first novel in the series, *Crossing the Continent*, is available from Talonbooks. Follow Talonbooks news for updates on the release of the next novel in the Desrosiers Diaspora series.

Born in a working-class family in Quebec, novelist and playwright Michel Tremblay was raised in Montreal's Plateau neighbourhood. An ardent reader from a young age, Tremblay began to write, in hiding, as a teenager. Because of their charismatic originality, their vibrant character portrayals, and the profound vision they embody, Tremblay's dramatic, literary, and autobiographical works have long enjoyed remarkable international popularity; his plays have been adapted and translated into dozens of languages and have achieved huge success throughout Europe, the Americas, and the Middle East.

A seven-time recipient of grants from the Canada Council for the Arts, during his career Tremblay has received more than sixty prizes, citations, and honours, including nine Chalmers Awards and five *Prix du grand public*, presented during Montreal's annual book fair, *Salon du livre*. Tremblay has also received six honorary doctorates.

The French Government, in 1984, honoured Tremblay's complete body of work when it made him *Chevalier de l'ordre des arts et des lettres de France*; thereafter, in 1991, he was raised to Officer of the Order. In 2008, he was created *Chevalier de la légion d' honneur de France*. Tremblay was appointed, in 1991, *Chevalier de l'ordre national du Québec*. In 1999, he received the Governor General's Performing Arts Award. In 2011, he was honoured with the *Révolution tranquille* medal, given by the Ministry of Culture of Quebec, awarded to artists, creators, and artisans who began their careers between 1960 and 1970 and who still have an influence in their field of practice.

ABOUT THE TRANSLATOR

Born in Moose Jaw, Saskatchewan, Sheila Fischman is a graduate of the University of Toronto. A co-founder of the periodical *Ellipse: Œuvres en traduction / Writers in Translation*, she has also been a columnist for the *Globe and Mail* and the Montreal *Gazette*, a broadcaster with CBC Radio, and literary editor of the Montreal *Star*. She now devotes herself full time to literary translation, specializing in contemporary Quebec fiction, and has translated more than 125 Quebec novels by, among others, Michel Tremblay, Jacques Poulin, Anne Hébert, François Gravel, Marie-Claire Blais, and Roch Carrier.

Sheila Fischman has received numerous honours, including the 1998 Governor General's Award (for her translation of Michel Tremblay's *Bambi and Me* for Talonbooks); she has been a finalist fourteen times for this award. She has received two Canada Council Translation Prizes, two Félix-Antoine Savard Awards from Columbia University, and, in 2008, she received the Canada Council for the Arts Molson Prize. She holds honorary doctorates from the Universities of Ottawa and Waterloo.